I want everything you have

Jenna O'Connor

1

This book is dedicated to all the woman who had no choice but to be strong.

To my mum, my sister, my gran and my best friend – I love you all and wouldn't have managed to do this without your support. X

Chapter 1

"Love you beautiful, Happy Birthday!" he said kissing my cheek and pulling me in close in front of all of our closest friends. "I love you too." I said kissing him back giddy with excitement and a little too much wine. Here we were on my twenty fifth birthday in our local Italian restaurant celebrating not only my birthday but great memories with great friends. I'd woken up this morning to a commitment ring from Damian; we have been together just under five years. We had begun our life journey together, a couple of years ago we'd bought a small property close by our home towns, we had a beautiful apartment, our puppy and we both have budding careers selling cars for Mercedes Benz, the world was our oyster.

The restaurant was crowded and stuffy, but we had taken over the main centre table. It was only our group that would be loud and lairy on a Friday night at 8pm in Bothwell.

Bothwell is my home it's a small town approximately thirteen miles from Glasgow. It is has been an up and coming area since the early nineties, professional footballers and successful middle-class businessmen began purchasing the houses in the area and since then the desirability of the area has grown. The streets were dotted with chic restaurants, small bars and boutiques. Bothwell was sometimes even been referred to as the Rivera of Glasgow. Beautiful wife's and girlfriends of the newly successful walking their dogs and pushing prams down the street after getting blow dry's in the main streets top salon. It wouldn't be abnormal to see a Bentley or Ferrari near Da lucianos, with everyone dressed to the nines screaming my life is better than your life. Luckily for me not everyone here is like that, the majority of people around were hard working middle class that have made it and want to enjoy life. They appreciate family life and quiet living but living well, and in Bothwell it definitely showed.

"Right everyone!" David shouted whilst standing up and holding his glass, "Who's coming to Vegas??" David is my sister Sophia's boyfriend. He works for an insurance company, he's one of two people either completely dead pan boring or life and soul of the party, who knows what it would be like in Vegas, only time will tell, at least we know a laugh is definitely guaranteed. 'We know you boring bastards aren't coming, looks like its Gabs, Damian, me, Soph, Euan and Emily. What about you guys? Tilly? Paddy?" he screamed across the table to the point people in the restaurant were looking.

"We would love to come." Tilly shyly replied, "Only if it is ok with everyone?"

Tilly and Paddy were the newest addition to our group; we met through Tilly's parents who had bought cars from us over the years. They owned a very successful construction company and were very close friends with Damian and I. We became friends with Tilly and Paddy as her parents always threw fantastic charity events where we would always be invited and from there got to know Tilly and Paddy.

Tilly was slightly younger but was quiet in nature, she didn't have a lot of friends but she was a nice girl and we had the same things in common. Paddy worked for Tilly's dad, he was good fun and got along with the boys brilliantly. Euan, well Euan was my best friend, we met a couple of years ago through Mercedes Benz and to be honest when we first met I hated him. He was a wealthy private school boy who acted like everyone had to bow down to him – I however am not that type of person. But after a while working together and bringing him down to where he should be I realized he wasn't all that bad, it was more of a façade. We became best friends and Euan brought Emily out with us most weeks.

Emily was his better half, she was as sweet as sugar, a makeup artist from the other side of Glasgow and looked like a princess, she always called you dolly and had the cutest voice to match her personality. We were the original members of our group.

"Babe, no way are they coming!" Emily whispered in the toilets, "they totally throw off the ambience; it's just getting too big a group, we don't need drama in Vegas, please tell David to shut up!"

"Don't worry doll, it'll be fine, they might not even come, let's just see what happens; we need to have a good night tonight, it's the first time I have been off on a Saturday in ageessss." I pulled her back into the restaurant desperate for another drink.

Not only do I have a really good group of friends I'd really hit the jackpot with Damian, he was tall, dark and handsome with piercing blue eyes. There's just me, him and our Chihuahua Penny starting the rest of our lives together.

"Last night was messy" Damian whispered in my ear.

"God, don't I know it, my head is pounding. David and those shots – god knows what him and Soph will have us like Vegas. We should start planning the dates so we can sort everything out and clear it with work."

"Of course Gabs, first time not going to Dubai, this is going to be interesting." He said getting up and walking into the kitchen.
I love it when he brings me tea to my bed, birthdays should last more than one day right? I don't even know what we should do today, see mum, or take Penny out, maybe some lunch? I should learn to sit still and enjoy the moment. I'm blessed with an active brain constantly planning and organizing – always trying to move forward, maybe I should learn to give my head a rest sometimes.

Our apartment was in a town three miles from Bothwell in a place called Hamilton, it was a two-bedroom conversion, with high ceilings and everything painted in crisp white. It had a large living room and a hallway which housed our magnificent wardrobe. When we moved in there was a fifteen-foot-long mirrored cupboard in the hall with nothing built into it, so of course we built a wardrobe – what else could you have possibly done with it? The windows were large and the space was bright and airy, we lived close to the centre of town; Hamilton was one of the slightly larger towns outside of Glasgow and just like everywhere else came with its good and bad spots. Cadzow Street was in between, close enough to the centre but far enough away from the not so nice areas. It was scary to think we had lived in our apartment for nearly three years, we had worked so hard for everything and what we have is the best of the best. Sometimes I think back to how we sat on the floor for six months whilst we waited on the custom white leather sofa. We were a bit crazy in that way, but we wanted nice things and if that meant we had to wait we did.

Damian and I loved holidays, we worked six days a week which worked out at nearly sixty hours most weeks, so it made sense to have amazing holidays and enjoy seeing the world together. In 2008 my grandparents took me to Dubai for the first time. I grew up a Disney child, always travelling back and forward to Florida when I was young, and as my sister and I got older we travelled to places like Spain and Greece. Dubai was the most magical place I had ever been, the golden desert and hot temperatures were exactly what I wanted. The buildings were beautiful and everything was fascinating. The luxury was like nothing I had ever seen. When Damian and I decided to go on our first holiday together it was right before Christmas, his suggestion was New York. I had been a few years before during my studies but never at Christmas time. Secretly I wanted to go to Dubai and the day Damian asked me if I would prefer New York or Dubai I couldn't hide my excitement. Since then we visited Dubai minimum once a year, it became a bit of a tradition for us. We worked our way through the five star hotels across Jumeriah; it was always the best time we spent together. Neither of us were stressed with work or targets and we could lie on the gorgeous beaches and enjoy each other's company, we scarified a lot for those moments together but they were always worth every second.

Four years ago, my mum took me to Las Vegas for my Twenty-first to see Celine Dion in the coliseum at Caesar's Palace. It was the most incredible concert I have ever seen. What an amazing talent and a memorable moment I got to share with my mum. We saw every theatre show across the Vegas strip, chilled at the hotel pools, shopped and learned how to play the slot machines. I was lucky to have a best friend in my mum. Damian however had never been to Vegas so when I suggested the holiday as a change to Dubai, he at first wasn't sure. We weren't a partying couple and didn't do the club scene very much. I researched a bit more and realized that there was so much more that you could do in Vegas which didn't mean constant clubbing. When we agreed on the location we both decided we should make it a group holiday, I knew this experience was not going to be one to forget.

G: 'Hey guys, were thinking the 24th of July 2014 until 4th of August? Probably better to fly from Manchester – Virgin? What do you think? X
David: I'm in whatever suits – Soph will be off, schools are out for the summer! Lucky bitch!

Damian: I'm good to go!

Emily: Ok guys let me and Euan sort it out and get back to you xxxx

Tilly: Were good to go! When will we book? And which hotel? X

Tilly was one of those lucky girls that worked 9-4pm for her dad and sauntered about in Louis Vuitton on a daily basis. Tilly was five foot six, with long dark hair exactly like me; she had greenish brown eyes and a small frame. She had a great body and looked after herself well; to be fair she had the money and the time on her side. I was a little jealous, I grafted my arse off I was still working towards the Louis, and the body of my dreams but whatever – I just need to keep telling myself material things don't make you a better person or give you a better life. Although I did wait six months for a customized sofa, but I suppose my priorities are different. I too was never one for staying in mediocre hotels but it would need to be something special if Tilly was coming. I can't imagine the places she's been with her family.

This was going to be an epic holiday. All of our closest friends were an amazing group of people. I just needed everyone to confirm the dates so we could confirm the hotel and begin to plan everything else we would do when we got there. Excited was a complete understatement.

Chapter 2

Just under four months to go, goals:

- Bikini body
- Sell min 15 cars per month
- Get blinds for the kitchen
- Buy ten bikinis
- Ten day/night outfits
- Find somewhere for Penny to stay while were in Vegas

Shut up brain! I need to go to work and focus on selling. Selling = all of this other stuff.

"Shorty, how many did you sell last week? In fact, how many did the big man sell?"

"shut up Rob, stop making it awkward!" Rob was the head valeter and long-term friend. He loved the banter and most of all creating competition between me and Damian.

"Even if I did do better it's ours anyways, so it doesn't make a difference who puts what in the pot." I replied giving him a shove. "But did you do better? That's what I asked?" Rob said laughing again. "Yes, but shush!" Damian and I shared everything we weren't one of those this is yours and this is mine type of couples. We were a team, but secretly I did love winning, sorry Damian, it's an Aries thing.

Working in a Glasgow showroom had its pros and cons, as did being the only female. I can be a bit of a diva at times but mostly I was one of the boys and was treated like one too. Every dirty joke and even every argument I was treated the same. I might always be wearing high heels and look like butter wouldn't melt but I have thick skin, it was the only way I could handle all the drama that comes with the job was to beat the boys. Every single last one of them, and I did month on month year on year. I loved my job and being successful was what made it so good. When people ask for "the wee lassie with the long dark hair" instead of "the forty-year-old bald man" it was always another point to Gabriella.

I remember being broke, no job, and I had left university. I was failing at life and my mum's patience was starting to run out. I had zero chance of getting a job in marketing or PR. It was a recession and what experience did I have? NONE. Off the cuff I thought it would be a good idea to sell cars, I mean how hard can it be, their clean, shiny and the showrooms are beautiful, I mean who wouldn't want to work in a fancy showroom. So, I applied for three jobs, BMW, Mercedes and an Arnold Clark motor store. Sadly, I never heard back from BMW, no wonder how does an Advertising and PR girl who dropped out of uni a month early get a job working for one of the biggest brands globally?

My interview at Arnold Clark was pretty funny, it was your typical motor store, cars everywhere with huge numbers screaming prices and offers for cars, balloons and bright colors and there were maybe twenty salesmen watching the pitch like lions awaiting their prey. The showroom was clean but worn, the desks were scattered everywhere and messy. As I walked into the manager's office I immediately felt nerves. I wasn't sure if it was nerves for the interview of nerves that I may actually work in this place, it wasn't really a Gabriella type place.

"You know you're gonna get your hair wet darling, you'll need to move cars in the rain." The manager said to me cheekily. Seriously? I mean is that not what umbrellas were invented for. What an Idiot! he was so patronizing but I needed a job. Funnily enough I got it on the spot – how I don't actually know, all I knew was my last car was black. I accepted the job but I just didn't feel like Arnold Clark motor store was my thing. I waited a few days and somehow I got a call from Mercedes. I couldn't believe it, there was no way that opportunity was ever going to happen twice.

My Gran and Grandad drove me to my interview and waited outside while I took my chance.

Mercedes Benz of Glasgow is a grand showroom dotted just off the motorway at the top of Glasgow city center. It was shiny and polished, every car was lined up in complete unison, the receptionists were glamorous and the showroom sparkled. When I was escorted into the conference room I was greeted by four managers, all in their thirties or forties in smart suits and striking ties. Clean shaven and smiling they questioned me one by one, each picking up on points the other had discussed and developing into more intense questions. I was twenty years old and had never been under this much pressure. I wanted this job, I could imagine myself working in this showroom and hopefully I could learn a thing or two as well as making some money to pay my student loan.

"Would you say listening is an important skill for sales Gabriella?" The main manager asked.

"Well yeah of course, you need to pay attention otherwise how would you know which way to lead the conversation?" I had no idea where he was taking this.

"Great, I am glad we agree. Can I ask you, what is my name?"

FUCK! I had no idea, his name, his name? My palms were sweating and I was hoping the chair would swallow me up. I laughed nervously digging out of this one would be hard, what on earth could I do other than tell the truth, here goes. "I am so sorry, I have absolutely no idea what your name is. I am so nervous and we have been speaking for about an hour, what I do know is his name is Matthew. But I can promise you one thing, I will never ever forget anyone's name ever again in my life. I am absolutely mortified." Luckily, they all laughed but on a serious note I was screwed, safe to say I would definitely not be getting a job in here. I nervously laughed as they went through their final questions secretly hoping the ground would swallow me up.

"So Gabriella, how do you think the interview went?" David the main manager asked me. I mean it's not like his name was even hard his name was Matthew, I should've known that.

"I think its went ok, minus the not remembering your name part. I am really hard working and my Gran and Grandad are waiting in the car outside for me, so I hope it's good cause they've got high hopes for me. "I was so nervous I was starting to shake. "How do you think it went?"

"We think it has gone very well, you seem very ambitious and you would be in a good position to be trained and taught the Stratstone way. One word of advice, we think you should change your email address, I mean ilovedesignershoes is great but it's not very professional." Ground swallow me up pleeeeeeeaaaaasssssseeeee, this is just getting worse.

Pep Talk! Ok so I do have a pretty embarrassing email address, but that's who I am. Why should I change my personality for a job? Que the quick answer.

"Thank you very much for your feedback, I do know where your coming from, but can I ask how many people applied for this position?" I was starting to get cocky and hopefully my arrogance would work out for the better.

"Around thirty." He replied confused.

"Thirty? So out of thirty CVs how many email addresses do you remember?" I had to pull this one out of the bag.

He laughed and chocked back his words. "Only yours" he looked shocked but he was smiling.

"Well it can't be that bad if you only remembered mine?" I laughed and they thanked me for my time. I swear that one line is what got me the job in there, and that is where I met Damian. He literally jumped down the stairs before I was called for my interview. Prada trainers, was what I saw first and he was tall, like really tall. Dark spikey hair, tanned and blue eyes, he was gorgeous and he looked right at me. I remember thinking I'd never pull a guy like that. Focus on getting a job Gabby, it was the last thing I had to think about, but there was definitely a moment.

Five years on we both work for Mercedes, he is in Giffnock showroom and I am in Glasgow. Sometimes I wonder what it would be like not working for the same company, however I'm glad we don't work for the same branch otherwise I'd be pulling my hair out, living and working together might get a bit much.

Chapter 3

"Babe, try virgin active? And bring in the Nando's sauce." Damian yells from the living room, sitting in the same spot on the floor. "Flipping Vegas is on, hurry up!"

Very much a creature of habit was my Damian, he'd come home from work, immediately undress and put his comfies on and sit on the same spot on the floor watching TV, he wasn't as lazy as he sounds he went to the gym 3/4 times a week and was always back and forward picking up penny and visiting the family. But this is the place I love the most, when we sit on the floor and eat our dinner watching crap TV; it's like our own little world. Maybe this weekend we can bring the mattress into the living room, drink wine and sleep on the floor, we loved doing stuff like that as simple as it sounds.

"I'm here, I'm here. There you go babe." I say passing the sauce. "I was thinking we should stay in the Aria, it's one of the newer hotels and it's really modern and stuff, it'll work out about one thousand seven hundred each which isn't too bad for ten days? What do you think?"

"Whatever makes you happy babe, I just want to see what it's like as a place. I hope it's everything you've said it'll be." He said tucking into his dinner.

G: Guys, direct flights from Manchester 24th of July until 4th of August staying in the Aria is one thousand seven hundred, shall we go ahead and book? X

Tilly: yeah sure! I'll transfer you the money! Send me your bank details and I'll send the money for me and Paddy! So excited! X

Euan: done, I'll give you the cash in work tomorrow! Cannie wait!!

Emily: Amazing Girls! We need a separate group chat to discuss outfits! Xxxxxxxx

Soph: no worries G, David will sort it with Damian. Good to go! X

Thank god that was it officially booked, at least we had something to work towards. As well as finalizing the holiday I've booked some of the classes at Virgin Active gym to see if that motivates me to go any more than normal.

Monday morning 7am, there was no way I was going to the gym on my own at that time, Damian grumpy from the early start headed for the weights and I went to head towards my class. Two people in the class! Jesus, I really am insane, I always knew no normal people get up and go to the gym at this time.

"Hey I'm Richie! I'm the trainer for this class, don't look so scared, this is Tom my mate it's just you two so it'll be more of a personal training session so just take it as it comes and we'll go from there."

"Is it that obvious I don't go to the gym?" he laughed and shook his head. "Ok let's see what this is about." I stood and watched/ tried to copy what he was doing, I am so out of my depth. I have never been a gym bunny. I know Vegas is calling but I don't know if I can humiliate myself like this. So after 40 minutes of lunging, crunching and pretending I was a lot more comfortable than I was, I signed up for personal training sessions with Ritchie. He was 21 and recently qualified; he seemed excited and happy to take on the challenge of awkward Gabriella. First thing on the plan to Vegas is in progress.

Chapter 4

The girls met at The Glasgow Fort – this was our local shopping centre. It was out door, which for Glasgow always having its cold and windy days seemed a bit crazy, but luckily it doesn't always rain – ok sorry it doesn't rain every hour of the day, just most of them. We sat down in Frankie and Bennies for some food and some serious Vegas planning.

"Girls I am so excited to pick our outfits and actually get there! What is everyone gonna bring?" I was so eager I couldn't wait to discuss; I was literally jittering in my seat.

"I think we should be cute and casual for travelling, like comfy joggies and stuff because it will be a hell of a long flight. " Emily suggested, whilst sipping her milkshake.

"Good shout Emily!" said soph. 'It's gonna be so long and were probably gonna be drunk. "Sophia says cackling away.

Part of me is excited and nervous to spend this amount of time with my sister, we are completely different people. Sophia is taller than me; she's five foot six and has middle brown hair, striking blue eyes and an extremely toned and trim physique. Her skin is pale and only takes a light tan whereas I am exactly like my dad, dark hair, and dark eyes and when I tan I change colour completely, we have the same mannerisms and since we were little, people would always ask if we are twins but we couldn't be more different if we tried. Personality wise Sophia is a vibrant and charismatic and she has a care free attitude about life and everything in it. Whereas I'm a highly-strung perfectionist/workaholic, I am five foot two and known as the runt of the family, usually gaining nicknames like shorty, wee yin, tiny, and short stuff, we couldn't be more opposite if we tried. I like working Sophia doesn't, I am not so good in the gym or exercise, Sophia is addicted, Sophia can party for days, I can party for minutes. But she is my sister and we should be able to do something spectacular like this together especially since there are just the two of us. I'm just not sure if it'll be a mistake, I don't want us to clash when everyone is there, and to be honest I don't know if I can keep up with the party girl status.

"I'm thinking dresses for night time and just little kaftans and swimwear for daytime, I got new Valentino sandals for the pool and my Louis beach bag but other than that I don't have anything else." Tilly stated whilst looking for approval. I'd better cut my Primark labels off my clothes before I go then, Jeez thank god Sophia and Emily are here; they'll keep things on the normality level.

"I think it'll be perfect honey!" I said looking at Tilly, "Soph I can't believe you got us Chippendales tickets for my birthday! Damian will kill you! – I suppose it gives the boys a reason to go to the strippers there too!" this is going to be an experience we won't forget."

Deep down I was ecstatic for the Chippendales, I wasn't really into this sort of thing, but if we are going to Vegas to have a once in a lifetime experience is this not one of the things you should do? The reviews were incredible, a show to remember, and comparing to the boys at least it was more of a show than a sleazy strip bar.

The bikini purchasing had started, five hundred pounds on Victoria's Secret bikini's and seventy pounds tax for delivery from America. What am I even doing? But if we're sitting with Miss Louis Vuitton at the pool I aint turning up like a tramp. I had planned my bikinis in perfect colour coordination to compliment my growing tan throughout the holiday. I bet none of the girls were as psychotic as me like this.

"I've got all my bikini's ready Dolly, mainly pink." Emily giggled. Emily was a proper fairy-tale princess again taller than me, probably the same height as the other girls, white blonde hair and gorgeous blue eyes. She has the body of a goddess and was so feminine, and not just in her looks in everything she did, her job, the way she spoke, the way she dressed, the way she carried herself. No wonder Euan was besotted by her she was such a perfect wifey, and that was exactly what he needed.

As the food came Sophia took charge of the conversation. "I think we should get dressed up most nights, it is Vegas and it is our holidays, plus we are gonna be partying so so hard!!" Sophia looked at me with a strange smirk on her face – we both knew this would be a test for me, I can practice partying surely?

The girls stuffed their faces with burgers and milkshakes and I couldn't help but think how lucky we were to all be friends, we had the crazy one, spoilt one, the princess and me the go getter. We were all so different but gelled all the same. Tilly and I were the most alike – we both have high expectations and always want the best. The only difference is Tilly can get whatever she wants from her dad and I need to work my backside off, we've all been dealt different cards I suppose. Emily and Sophia are more of the same; they want to settle down get married and have babies, they don't really care about careers, they would rather have the simple things.

We were planning the holiday of a lifetime, Calvin Harris at Wet republic, Chippendales, Red foo at the Encore, the High roller, maybe even a show, plus there were dinners and casino nights. We had to go see the Venetian and have a ride in the Gondolas. There was too much to even think about. I loved Vegas and since my twenty-first it was my second favourite place in the world after Dubai, I couldn't wait to show Damian what it was like, the people, the casino's the heat, the atmosphere. Vegas is an electric place and I was so bored of work and rain, this was a perfect experience for us before we move onto the next stage of our lives.

The girls and I agreed to glam up and keep in touch about the progress of our purchases, in the lead up to the holiday.

Chapter 5

I couldn't stop looking at my ring, it was Swarovski and sparkly. It wasn't overly expensive or an engagement ring. It was a simple Swarovski band, small and delicate, perfect for me. The point of this is that he gave it to me, and he is telling me this is it, it's us against the world. We lay in bed half snoozing and chatting about life, all I can think of is how much I love this man.

"Baby, we need to plan ahead." Damian said.

"Yeah? What you thinking?"

"What do you think of the Royal Meridien?"

"What in Dubai? Can we get Vegas over with first before we book another holiday?" I questioned him; we had already spent a small fortune.

"Maybe we should get married in Dubai? Like no fuss or any big huge get together just the people we want to be there? What do you think?" he said looking at me as if I already knew his thoughts. I could picture it now, sandy beaches, crystal champagne glasses, and the stunning sunset across the Arabian Gulf, in the most intimate setting – Damian and I with our family and closest friends. We would have our toes in the sand. Me with a simple and elegant gown, something lace or fitted with a trailing fish tail. Damian would wear a white open shirt and white linen chinos. I swear I can smell the roses and lilies when I think about this moment. It would be so perfect, like something out of a movie. This would be a dream come true. "I think that sounds perfect!" I yelped trying to contain my excitement; but should we really skip a proper engagement and plan a wedding? I don't think that is how the fairy-tale normally goes?

"Who would we invite though?" I tried to act cool as secretly my heart flipped and I was filled with so much happiness. He wants to plan our wedding. Ok so we're not engaged, but oh my god it's going to happen. Breathe Gabriella, chill out. He's not proposed, yet – eeekk.

"Ahh you see that's the hard bit, not many from my side, mum, dad, sister, niece, who else. Ben, Katrina, Jason, Louise? That sounds about it? Andrew won't come his Mrs. won't allow him and we don't want her there." he chuckled.

"Hmmm who would we ask? Mum, Sophia, David, Gran, uncles? Aunties, welsh family? God there's a lot more than we thought, Julia? Who else would we need to ask?" I had to make a list, but should I plan my wedding guest list without a ring?

"Make a note on your phone of all the people and we'll look at the money, I'm sure the families will help out a little too." he grinned.

"Do you think we'll actually do this?" I asked with nervous excitement.

"I fucking hope so." he said kissing me. "It's more us? You not think?"

"It sure is, I always wanted to have my toes in the sand when I get married." I wonder if he heard my thoughts or maybe I've slipped into conversation once or twice before.

"What? No shoes? That will save some money ha ha." he answered snuggling into me and kissing my face.

"You're not getting away with it that easy, I want shoes of course; very very special shoes, I just had an idea in my head I'd have my toes in the sand while we said our vows. I liked the feeling of my feet in the sand; it makes me feel really calm."

"That sounds like a very good idea little monkey, I like It." he said grabbing me. "Right are we gonna leave the house today? Or shall we just stay in bed? We haven't done that in ages? We can get a Bombay Cottage tonight if you want?" mmm Butter chicken sounds exactly like what I need.

"That sounds perfect!" A day in bed with my gorgeous man, and we've just decided that were gonna get married in Dubai, my head is totally in the clouds.

"Right come here you!" he said kissing me. "I love you." He said looking deep into my eyes.

"I love you more." I whispered.

Looking back I don't know how it happened, but as soon as I got the job in Mercedes my life went from zero to hero. Everything fell into place, the man, the house, the puppy, and now "the ring" well ring to be. We had so much still to do before we have babies, although I have dreamt that I have three boys towering over me exactly like their dad, they'd come and chat to me and give me hugs whilst I stand in the kitchen and make them dinner – I should really learn how to cook first before this actually happens otherwise I'll be putting frozen meals in the microwave. They would be going out with their dad playing football and being good to their little mum. I could think about it all day, I didn't ever think it would ever feel so strong about a person or love something so much, but here I am looking at my Swarovski ring like I've won the lottery, and literally no one is taking me off this cloud.

Chapter 6

"Hello Gabriella speaking."

"Hi, this is Raymond from Porsche Glasgow, is this Gabriella?"

"Hi, yes this is Gabriella, how can I help you?"

"I'm calling as one of our long-term salesmen retired. We now have an opportunity at Porsche and we think you would be the right person for the position. What do you think?"

Oh My God! I can't believe this is happening, Porsche Glasgow? Me? What did I think? I think I know absolutely nothing about Porsche; I don't even like manual cars, is there a point in changing jobs right now? I need to speak to Damian. How do I even handle this?

"Thank you so much for calling me, I am really honoured you even thought of me to be honest. I wasn't planning on changing brands, I am really comfortable at the moment . . . you've actually caught me off guard and I really don't know what to say."

"That's no problem at all." Raymond said, "I would appreciate if you would visit the showroom to discuss the options further."

"em . . . yeah ok, well let me speak to my partner first and I will get back to you." I stammered through my words and tried to act cool. Deep down I was crapping myself.

"Damian? Yeah of course Gabriella, it's a fantastic opportunity for you and I'm confident you will be happy with the package and direction of the brand. This is my direct number, so please give me a call back. I hope to hear from you soon. Bye." And just like that he hung up.

I think I need to sit down, little Gabriella from Bothwell was just offered an opportunity at Porsche Glasgow! How do they even know who I am? I mean I know one of the boys over there that used to work in Mercedes, maybe that was the link? I'm not really a petrol head kind of girl, maybe Damian would know more about this, he'll know what to do, should I change?

Pick up pick up pick up! This man honestly! Where is he when you need him!

"Hey baby, what's up?" Damian answered cheerily.

"Oh my god, Oh my god, Oh my god, Oh my god!" I was literally shrieking on the phone.

"Oh my god, what??? What the hell is it?" he panicked, I must've been over exaggerating again.

"I have just been invited to Porsche Glasgow to discuss a position!!!!" he would probably have disowned me if he seen that victory dance.

"Porsche . . . really. . . wow? That's unexpected. Well, congratulations babe, you have been working hard. . . I mean do you want to work in a place like that? Is it maybe too much engine focused for you?" he seemed a bit quiet, and puzzled by my excitement. To be fair I don't know why I was so excited, maybe it was recognition for my hard work, at least was finally paying off.

"I don't even know what I think, but it is really amazing though; that they even know who I am In the first place, I think you know the guy Raymond? Did you not work with him before?" please just back me up here Damian. "Yeah we did, he's a good guy, heard he's done very well for himself there. I'm mega busy today so I'll call you soon. Love you." Before I even replied he'd hung up too, what is it with men and phones.

Was that an odd reaction? Or is he actually happy for me? God I'm so overwhelmed do I move or not? I do love my job and I'm at the peak of my career here, I'm hoping I'll be promoted within the next year. But is it time to better myself and move forward, I'm gonna message Billie, she'll be proud of me.

Billie is one of my closest friends that I used to work in Mercedes as part of the reception team. She is one of the most thoughtful and caring people I have ever met. A couple of years ago she decided to spread her wings literally and move to Dubai to work for Emirates. What a job she had, I love when she sends me snaps of her travels – the Trevi fountain, New York, Christmas on the beach, brunches honestly she has it all, and seeing as Damian and I love Dubai so much we get to cross paths a few times a year whether she is there or we are here. Speaking of Billie we are actually overdue a catch up, now that I think of it.

G: What's new B?? I have goss. x

Billie: I've literally just woken up from a flight, goss, what goss? Are you and Damian????xxxxxxxxxxxxxxx

G: God no lol! Were only Swarovski commitment ringing it just now, poor guy – I must be setting my standards too high he's shitting himself. LOL x
B: awww man, I want to be a bridesmaid, hurry up already!!! Xxxxxxxxxxxxxxx

G: well we've finally booked Vegas, YAY!!! And . . . x

B: and . . .xxxxxxxxxxxxxxx

G: Porsche called and want to discuss a position with me!!!!x

B: Shut up!! That is fucking amazing doll!! I knew something like that would happen to you. You are un real! That is so good! So when are you going? What's happening!! What did Damian say? Xxxxxx

G: well I don't know yet I said I would call them back, do you think I should go meet them? X

B: Defo babe, your granddad always said better yourself if you can and I'm pretty sure this counts as bettering yourself!! Xxxxxx

G: it's probably worth a meeting, we'll see what Damian says tonight, he knows more about this sort of stuff than me, how's James? All ok? X

B: James is good babe, were gonna wait a while before we get married and plan something awesome. Your dress is still happening though don't you worry! Xxxxxxxxx

G: Good because I still want my bridesmaid duties!! Ill message you soon and let you know the chat x

B: Love you doll xxxxx

G: love you x

Well if Billie says it's good it must be, mum and Gran seem keen enough, this may potentially worth taking the risk and changing, I just need to figure out where Damian stands with this, I can't make the decision without him.

Chapter 7

We had 8 weeks until Vegas, and the excitement was growing. Euan agreed to have a BBQ at his new place so everyone could spend a bit of time together as a group before we all went away. Then we had planned Sophia's birthday, and then there would be the pre Vegas hangover style party at ours! Unfortunately Paddy couldn't make it to Euan's BBQ, so we brought Tilly along so she could mix with the girls and get comfortable socializing with everyone.

"These hoes aint loyal! These hoes aint loyal!" Sophia chanted and started doing this amazing hip hop dance in the middle of the living room floor. The boys stood outside fumbling around with a throw away BBQ whilst we poured the drinks and chatted inside. His new place was gorgeous; it was a small duplex apartment about ten miles away from us. It had a bachelor type feel to it although Emily's pink fluffy blankets and accessories seemed to be found dotted around the place.

"Sophia can you teach me how to do that too? I mean us. We could so do this dance in Vegas." Emily started to copy Sophia. "Gabby come on!" I was not a dancer. Well I can move, but it was a bit advanced for me, after Sophia repeated the dance fifty million times I managed to remember it. Although I didn't look like her when I did it I certainly gave it a good go. Where is Tilly? We were so preoccupied dancing I didn't even realize she was helping with the BBQ outside, at least she's getting to know everyone. As we practiced Damian came back into the house.

"What are you guys doing?" Damian laughed getting the wine from the fridge and pouring me a glass.

"Damian shusht! We're practicing our dance moves for Vegas!" I giggled.

"THESE HOES AINT LOYAL!" Sophia screeched in his face. "We are so doing this dance when we get to Vegas!" To be fair it was a really good song, and if we could all dance like Sophia it would be epic.

"Ha ha, right ok. Just don't hurt yourself. Are you coming outside for food?" he said gesturing me outside with my glass of wine.
Euan started plating out the burgers and hot dogs, whilst Emily organized the salad. Tilly was standing really close to Euan; it did look a little bit cozy, but it wasn't the biggest garden so I'm sure it wasn't intentional, she was only trying to get along with everyone in the group.

Euan had brought some of his school friends to the BBQ, the garden was crowded and the house was sprinkled with empty glasses. I began tidying up, it was a Saturday night and we all had to work in the morning, all meaning me, Euan and Damian, either way the house was a still a complete mess and I didn't fancy putting up with Euan in a grumpy mood all day tomorrow.

Sophia sat on the couch guzzling her last wine chuckling with David. "Guys, where's Emily?" I asked.

"Dunno sis, haven't seen her in ages?" Sophia replied looking around, "is she in the bathroom? Maybe check there?"

I chapped the door praying Emily was inside. "Emily babe? Are you in there?"

"Yes dolly." She sounded solemn.

"Is everything ok?" I could tell she wasn't ok. Putting my ear to the door she opened it slowly and invited me in.

"no." she wiped her tears, "not at all, I've been in here for forty-five minutes and Euan hasn't even looked for me."

"aww babe, don't say that. I'm sure that's not the case, people have been leaving and he was standing in the garden beside the barbeque. He's just entertaining. I've been washing glasses and putting everything in the trash, the place was a bit of a mess. . ."

"No Gabby! That's not it Tilly has been literally hanging off him all night. She has been constantly touching him, laughing at his jokes, standing directly beside him; she literally has not let his side since the second she got in here. She didn't even learn the dance!" Emily was distraught; I wiped her mascara and gave her a hug.

"Ok babe, I'm not going to lie and say I didn't notice I did. But I don't think it's intentional, she doesn't have many female friends and maybe she just gets on with the boys better. She probably doesn't know who to turn to because Paddy isn't here. It won't be intentional, look were all gonna head home soon anyway. So let's dry your tears and wipe your face and we'll have one more wine and I'll get her out of your hair how does that sound?"

"It better be a strong drink than a wine then." She replied smirking. "That's the lady I know. Come on princess go back and give your man a kiss."

We walked back through to the kitchen and poured two vodka and cranberries. We cheered to a phenomenal friendship and to Vegas. Emily was such a lovely person and I couldn't help but feel bad that she would feel insecure about something so trivial. Tilly had definitely over stepped the mark but surely it's because Paddy wasn't there. Maybe I should have a little chat with her and try to guide her the right way; she was only twenty-one she obviously didn't realize what she was doing.

Chapter 8

Resigning from Mercedes wasn't as hard as I initially thought. I mean they didn't want me to leave, but they did finally accept it and gave me a couple of weeks' notice. Mercedes was an amazing place to work, the brand itself was phenomenal, and it had been a hard few years of work, but I was grateful for everything I learned, it was a shame I was outgrowing the job but I needed to change and work on my skill set. Porsche would do exactly that for me, I can't say I wasn't scared but I wanted to at least take the chance.

I had a couple of weeks to settle and begin my training before we went to Vegas. Porsche was a family. Everyone was there for each other and they had a great friendship in the office. It was a different approach everyone helped each other, we were competitive but everyone was winning separately and also as team. Raymond our manager always made sure we all spent time together and socialized as friends, I felt like I knew everyone for years, it was the perfect fit. All I had to do was use this chance and make it work, just like Mercedes although with better tools to do the job this time. Driving my new Audi A5 coupe to work felt strange. I felt weirdly older and more mature, my granddad I'm sure would be proud of me. I could speak to upper class people? I could learn about sports cars and I could definitely transfer my skills from Mercedes Benz to Porsche. Although I may forget sometimes I am Gabriella Johnson and although I look cute, I have the ability and determination to make this work no matter what happens, the first step training down at Silverstone.

"Well monkey, enjoy your training and I'll see you in three days." Damian said kissing me in the morning before I left.

"Ok Mr, love you."

"Love you more."

Porsche training was another level; everyone already knew each other and had proper working relationships between the dealerships. They were focused and the classes weren't too big, they split the training fifty per cent driving and fifty per cent classroom. There were never more than thirty people training there at any one time. I was out of my depth technically, but at least I could interact with people. So far, I felt more connected to these people here than I ever did in Mercedes. It was weird but comforting. Sean and Sam were attending it with me and luckily being the only female I could sleep in the back of the car while they took turns driving down to Silverstone.

"What time are we meeting for dinner?" Sean said as we checked into the hotel. "Say in an hour an hour and a half?"

"Sounds good guys, see you soon."

I unpacked my case and organized my clothes for the next few days' worth of training.

"Hi babe, I'm just letting you know I'm here and just wanted to remind you to pick up Penny at my mum's after work."

"Ok darling, I'm just in work, gonna go for a beer with the boys after work. But I'll go get her later don't worry."

"That's ok, have you sold anything today?"

"Yeah we've done a few. Showroom is busy though so got to go. Enjoy your dinner tonight and I'll message you later, love you."

"Love you."

I have just enough time to have a nap and then meet the boys down stairs. Training didn't officially start until tomorrow so a few glasses of wine and an early bed sounds perfect.

It was a typical English four star hotel that most companies would use, it had the usual brick style walls and bar area with offers on beer plastered on the walls. There were a few TVs showing the latest football game and a slot machine in the corner. The menu was filled with, roast beef, sausage and mashed potatoes, Sheppard's pie, chicken pie. Basically any kind of pie you'd like, as the boys cheered on the football I drank my wine quietly. It was a strange feeling to be able to sit in the one place without watching the clock or rushing to where I need to be next.

"You ok Shorty?" Sam asked glugging his beer, "another on Sean?" four beers down and they were happy as larry.

"I'm ok for now; don't think I can keep up with you guys."

"Just order her one; we'll claim it back anyways. So little princess how's life? You're all settled with big Damian, the handsome fucker he is . . . he's good banter that guy. I worked with him for a couple of years at Mercedes. Before your time wee darling. He used to know that guy, what's his name again. Worked up near his way. . ."

"Yeah I totally know who you mean! Ha ha, NOT!"

"Just phone him."

"Ok then. . . .Hey babe, I'm sitting with Sean and Sam and they said you know a guy can I pass you over to them?"

"I'm just driving to get Penny I'll call later if that's ok. See you soon monkey" and he clicked the phone down.

"Aw ok then. See you soon Mr." Weird It was nearly 10pm, it was late to be going to get Penny.

"Shorty, what did he say? There's your wine."

"Thank you, he's driving he said he'll call back later."

"Aw ok darling. Not that it matters anyways."

Four wines down and I am ready for bed. How can I even drink this much? The bar was spinning around me, I'm patiently awaiting the hangover from hell, training will be a struggle but at least I don't need to drive in the morning.

"I'm off to bed guys, enjoy the rest of the night."

"Give us a hug Shorty. Sweet dreams see you at seven thirty. Don't be late." Sean said and winked at me.

All I could think of was downing a bottle of water and falling asleep. Those boys are hard core, after two days of training and classroom I was in a far better position to take on my new sports car fanatic role, I never thought I'd like the track and driving but it was absolutely amazing I had really caught the buzz for it, everything was coming together nicely and there was only a few weeks now till Vegas – excited much?

Chapter 9

"There's no way that you are going to wear that!" Damian scowled at me; it was so hot and in the middle of June, I thought the short baby pink Zara dress deserved an appearance.

"What do you mean?" I asked shocked.

"You can see your backside, you look tacky." Damian walked into the kitchen to get a drink as he left me standing alone looking in the mirror in the hallway. Where the hell did that come from? Who does he even think he is speaking to?

When you invest in a 15ft long wardrobe you'd think you had clothes readily available for wearing at the drop of the hat. I wonder what he deems as acceptable to go out in. It was one of Glasgow's hottest summers and I was warm and stuffy. With my patience now gone I needed a plan B. Emily and Euan will be here soon; and I'm running out of time before we need to leave for Sophia's birthday drinks I only have half an hour. What the hell am I going to wear? I was getting agitated.

"Damian? Did you really need to say that?" he clearly wasn't listening. "Damian!" I screamed at him from the hallway.

"What is it Gabby!! For fuck sake, I gave you my opinion, so can you put some clothes on please!"

I don't know what has gotten into him. He is so mean, don't cry, don't cry Gabriella. It's hard to have a private meltdown when your wardrobe is in your hallway which is connected to your front door. Sadly, I had a face that showed every emotion and unfortunately for me Euan and Emily were already standing in our hallway before I had time to fix the situation on my face. You couldn't have planned this awkward moment any better.

"Hiya darling, how is everything? . . . Are you not ready yet?" Euan said mid hug coming through the front door. I needed to try and save face. Hugging him back, "No pal, not yet, having a little female moment but I just need to change and I'm ready other than that."

"Good, Emily go help her, Damian get the drinks poured!" the boys walked away and Emily and I are left in the hallway, silent. I knew she could tell we'd had words. But I wasn't going to bring it up; if I talked about it I would definitely have a breakdown.

"Ok Dolly, let's see what you have, what about these cute shorts with the black strappy platform heels and the pink chiffon top? Done!" Sometimes Emily just got it, she totally saved the day. I wasn't in a shorts mood but I was out of options. So I put the outfit on and we all headed into town. Damian and I never acknowledged each other until we reached the bar. "Feel better now?" he asked.

"Yeah I'm fine, does this look better?" I said sarcastically.

"Yes Gabby, you look gorgeous. Can we get over it and have a good night now?" he smirked cheekily.

"Ok Mr." he kissed me and we walked to Sophia's table.

Sophia was never one for over the top lavish bashes, she preferred a student pub with pool tables and cheap booze, and here we were in the centre of Glasgow in a basement bar with all of Sophia's closest friends. Paddy couldn't make it this event either so Tilly came on her own to mingle with the group a bit more before the holiday, the more time we all spent together the better. Ten days would be a long time with four couples. As always Sophia looked gorgeous and cool at the same time, in a bright pink top and skorts co-ord. How does she make something gorgeous look cool, FML I need a drink, I didn't look terrible but I didn't feel with it at all.

Sophia's friends were a lot of fun; we were all drinking and dancing, twirling each other around the dance floor whilst the boys drank and played pool. As usual David was drunk and causing mayhem. "Damian babe, can you go to the bar and get us some drinks it's so busy and my feet are hurting." I didn't want to fight with him, he was probably looking out for me anyways I mean I didn't want strangers to see my ass anyways. We could make up properly later when we went home.

"Ok, monkey" he said and kissed me and walked to the bar.
I thought it was best to sit with Sophia's work mates, try and relieve the pain from my feet for a bit. Around half an hour had passed and I realized I still don't have a drink. Where the hell is he? Thank god he's a tall man, I can see his head sticking over the crowd, and it looks like he's been fighting his way to the front of the bar. That's my guy, how could I ever be mad at him, he's only trying to keep me classy, and it's only a Zara dress. Worse things could happen.

"GiGi my gorgeous girl!! How are you?????" slurring his words Andy my sisters gay best friend and our hairdresser lay across me. "I am so happy to see your pretty face!" he said hugging me tightly. Andy was clean cut, perfectly groomed and one of the best dressed men you will ever see, some would call it a waste, he was one of the nicest people you could meet and one hell of a hairdresser. "You'll never guess what I just did, literally and I mean literally walked up to the bar and I saw Damian chatting away to a girl with long dark hair like you, I mean it as your actual double, and I walked up to her and felt her arse. Mwahahaha can you believe I actually did that" He was howling with laughter. "I mean I was fucking mortified it wasn't even you! It was that Tilly bird, they've been standing there for ages." I mean Tilly resembled me a little bit, but not really, there were clear differences. I couldn't see Tilly from where I was standing, but why was he standing at the bar talking to Tilly? "I think they've had a drink or two there." Andy giggled he was tipsy. I mean he has only been gone forty minutes, and the bar was busy maybe he was just getting me a drink like he said he was.

I waited quietly for another twenty minutes and all of a sudden felt really sad. I couldn't sit there with Sophia's friends laughing and joking, they were all smashed and I was stone cold sober. I walked to the ladies bathroom and shut myself into a cubicle. Surely he didn't fight with me then stand at the bar all night with another girl. I mean not that Tilly would ever do that, but it's just the principle of it all. Why is Damian so agitated with me? Or why am I so agitated with him? Was this a coincidence?

"Gabby babe? are you in here??" Emily comes into the toilet shouting merrily. "Yeah babe, I'm just coming out" I say wiping my tears; I didn't want to explain to anyone. It was Sophia's birthday now was not the time or the place. I was working tomorrow It was probably best I headed home.

"You ok my wee dolly?" she said hanging on me drunkily. "Yeah of course babe" I gave her a hug and washed my hands.

"You want to see Tilly she's wasted." Emily danced her way back to Sophia and the girls and I looked for Damian and Tilly. Wasted? Was he not waiting for a drink for us? That's strange?

He was nowhere to be seen. Where the fuck was he? I was starting to panic. "G ! Come and sit with us" Euan and David yell at me. "How's my sistaaaa? You look like you've seen a ghost?" David screeched as the two of them staring at me whilst smoking just outside the front door next to the exit stairs. It was three am and it was raining lightly.

"Where's Damian?" I asked.

"Don't sweat it he walked Tilly upstairs to get a taxi she's really drunk you know." David smiled cheekily.

They're upstairs? Alone? Why? Is that normal? Am I over reacting? I walked upstairs and they were perched on a wall, Tilly did not seem like she was on this planet.

"God sake Damian, what will we say to her mum and dad? Tilly is younger than us we shouldn't be getting her like that! How do we explain this?" This was embarrassing, if they knew she might not even be allowed to come to Vegas.

"Right, let's just get her in a taxi and drop her home." Damian said as he flagged a taxi and strapped her on the seat, I couldn't speak I was livid. He obviously thinks I'm an idiot standing there waiting for my boyfriend to buy me a drink while he stands chatting to another girl. If the shoe was on the other foot I would be a dead woman.

"Gabby! I really love you loads, you really are such a good girl. Honestly. . . I can't even say. I just love you both loads. "Tilly was smashed and slurring her words. She rolled around the seat as the driver swooped through the traffic as we left town.

She better not be sick in this taxi. All we need to do is to get her home and into bed, I'll figure out how to deal with him later. Damian stayed quiet through the taxi ride, and I just answered Tilly when appropriate throughout her outbursts, luckily Tilly was unaware of the awkwardness.

"Gabby! Gabby!!!!!!!!! GABBBBBBYYYYYYYYYYYY! I love you? Do you know that? I actually love you!! And I just . . . I . . . I . . . I want everything you have!" and she sat with a big smile on her face.

I laughed and stroked her head, "don't be silly darling, I don't know anyone that wants to work sixty hours a week and look after a man and a dog. Silly sausage, were just normal people trying to make a good life for ourselves. You and Paddy will have that one day I'm sure." I said uneasily. What a weird thing to say? By that point she'd dosed off. Who the hell says something like that? Is that normal? She's obviously just drunk.
We dropped her home and I made sure she got in the door safe. The thought of her parents seeing her like that stressed me out, Damian and I

still were not in a talking mood; you could cut the tension with a knife, so we sat the taxi journey home in silence.

As we walked into the house I couldn't help myself. "You do know you went to get me a drink nearly 3 hours ago now?" I snarled at him.
"Give me a break G I was being nice, Paddy wasn't there and she was a bit overwhelmed by Sophia and all her friends. You know what their like. Let's get changed and we can chill in the living room for a bit."

I did not want to chill, we had work in the morning and I was sober, upset about my outfit and tired. "Come here? Come and sit beside me Gabby? No need to be like that. I'm only trying to make it easier for when everyone goes away. How would you feel walking into our group if you didn't know anyone and you didn't have me?" I didn't want to reply.

"Gabby! I know you know what I'm saying; you wouldn't want anyone to be left out. Sophia's friends are all crazy and a bit you know over powering. She is a bit uncomfortable with girls. Just give her time; she's trying to find her place in the group."

He did have a point; it is nice to be nice. Although who says I want everything you have? It's not like she said that's a nice top where did you get that? That is 100% the weirdest thing anyone has ever said to me? I think I need to call my mum; Damian is obviously ignoring this point.

Chapter 10

Sunday mornings were slightly easier than every other day of the week. We both start work late and could get a mini lie in and have a proper breakfast together. Penny would snore at the bottom of our bed and although she can't speak I know she appreciates the extra hour in bed with her mum and dad. During the weekday's she would go to my mum's office and play there so the down time was appreciated by her. Our hours were too long to leave her home alone all week, so it worked out perfectly.

"Have I told you lately that I love you . . ." Damian sang kissing me on the head. "Have I told you there's no one above you, FILL MY HEART WITH GLADNESS TAKE AWAY ALL MY SADNESS, EASE MY TROUBLES THATS WHAT YOU DO." Damian sung in his worst impression singing voice.

"Damian," I said laughing, "come here you!" Not only did we have breakfast on a Sunday, it was cheesy Sunday song day. We would pick our favorite old songs and sing them to each other. We got to the point where sometimes we would just do it off the cuff.

"Ok! My turn! . . . mmmmm yeah . . . looks like we made it, look how far we've come my baby, we mighta took the long way, we knew we'd get there someday. They said I bet, they'll never make it but just look at us holding on. . . were still together still going strong." Who didn't love Shania? Que the moment being ruined.

"Babe, I need some white t shirts for holidays, I was thinking for with my shorts at the pool, maybe five white and five black?" Damian looked at me with his puppy dog eyes, he obviously wanted me to go pick them up for him.

"You're still one I run to, the one that I belong to, you're still the one I want for life, you're still the one I love the only one I dream of . . . "trust him to cut me off mid flow. I love that song.

"Do you want me to go after work?" I asked. It was Sunday and since I moved to Porsche my hours were very slightly better than his. I worked 12-4pm whilst he worked 11-5pm. I mean it was right beside the showroom I don't see why I wouldn't go for him, I suppose I could always pick up a few bits and pieces for me too.

"Can you? It would make it so much easier tonight and we can chill and watch homeland later?"

"Ok then, I'll do that then pick up Penny and meet you at the house later. What size do you want me to get?" Damian was 6ft 4, he had broad shoulders but he wasn't a big guy, as in width. Some would have called him lanky but he had a good body, minimal fat, abs and good arms. However, that never helped when he needed something to wear sometimes it was small and sometimes it was medium.

We looked at the t shirts in his cupboard and agreed medium was the best option, he had been working out a lot for the holiday so would probably need the bigger size. I couldn't lie and say I didn't love his new obsession with the gym, he looked amazing.

Work flew in, there was customers everywhere and I was rushing to get the shops, I got there by 5pm and went straight to Topman. Five white and five black medium T shirts, V neck collar, Easy peasy, I better be getting a reward for being such a good girlfriend.

"Hey Soph, I just thought I'd call to say hi, I'm in Buchanan Galleries and I thought I would give you a call before I head home."

"Hey, I'm alright sis, what are you getting?" She asked.

"Just t shirts for Damian, then I'm gonna have a look around for myself. I need some Sandals. Any ideas?"

"Why don't you try river island they had some nice ones, and some bikinis?"

"Yeah good plan, I need some sunglasses but I am hopefully going to hit my target and I'll get some vouchers for Frasers so I can get something decent."

"You deserve it G, new job and you've been working so hard. Just don't lose them like the last time. What are you doing tonight?" she chuckled.

"Nothing much, I just need to finish up here, pick up Penny and then head home for some dinner. I think we might get a takeaway and watch homeland. Sometimes I don't know how I fit it all in."

"You always fit in though, I have prep for dancing this week so David is going to watch the football and give me some peace and quiet to plan the next show. Well enjoy your night. I need to get off the phone and get working. Talk soon." She clicked the phone off and I decided to head home, it was nearly 6pm, I still hadn't considered the traffic or picked up Penny. The things you do the please your man.

I couldn't help but think about Sophia was I was driving home, she was an amazing dancer, she was so meticulous with her movements and had perfect timing, we both danced since we were two years old, I mean I can hold a beat but I'm not half as good as Sophia. Every show the family would come to, they would say - oh Sophia that was amazing, you were so fantastic, and Gabriella. . . Well done, you did good. I didn't let it bother me, I was more into singing. Every week I would sing in clubs across Glasgow with my grandad watching me, it feels like a distant memory sometimes. But since he passed I just don't feel like it's the same anymore. The most you'll get out of me is a song for a special birthday in the family or a full-blown concert when I'm in the shower. That normally happens on my day off when Damian is at work. I wish I could be as vibrant and care free as Sophia, and I really hope we get on together on this holiday.

By the time I got home it was nearly 7pm. Traffic was a nightmare and my mum was going on and on. I just wanted to put my pajamas on and relax. I struggled upstairs with the bags filled with t shirts, my new sandals, the takeaway and the dog. When I opened the door, Damian had assumed the normal position on the floor leaning his back on the couch.

"Did you get the t shirts?" he asked.

"Yeah, I got them," I put the takeaway in the kitchen and the bags in the bedroom. Damian bounced into the bedroom to try everything on. Once I'd changed I plated up our dinner.

"I didn't realize how hungry I was." Bombay cottage genuinely had the best curries on our side of the city. This would certainly make up for my stressful afternoon, I poured a glass of wine and zoned out for a second whilst I had my first taste.

"Babe, it's too big!" Damian yelled.

"What's too big hun?" I shouted back, after I jumped out of my skin.

"Eh, the t shirt, look at the state of this?" he walked into the kitchen pulling the t shirt from side to side, I mean it's not fitted at all?" he huffed and puffed looking at me.

"That's ok, the receipt is in the bag, we can just do an exchange." I took another gulp of wine and sat back in the chair. Another thing back on my never-ending list.

"When are you gonna take it back?" Damian, I suppose was referring to me taking it back at this point.

"I'll do it in the week hun, we've got time don't worry."

"Can you not do it tomorrow? I don't want to leave it late and I can't get the one I want."

"Ok I can go tomorrow; can you pick up Penny after work for me then?" I shouted through to the hallway to him.

"No, I don't have time, I'm going to the gym." he replied.

"Ok then." I need another glass of wine. This was becoming a habit, two glasses of wine and bed, not exactly following the Vegas diet but I was stressed out of my head. The wine went down a treat, all I had to do was change the t shirts over, and pick up the dog tomorrow, it's not even an issue. How could we go looking like slobs?

Chapter 11

Tilly: Babe, are you coming to this event on Friday? Xxx

G: yeah, I think so, did Paddy say to Damian? X

Tilly: Yeah, he said you guys were coming. I can't wait to see you Hun xxx
G: I know I think I'm going to wear my white peplum dress, have you decided what to wear yet? X

Tilly: I'm going to wear my new black bandage dress. Btw I got my hair done at that place you go to. My extensions are amazing. I absolutely love them. I cut them like yours, I hope you don't mind. XXX

G: of course, babe she's really good isn't she? X

Tilly: she's amazing! Can't wait to see you!!!!!! XXX

G: See you Friday babes x

Tilly's mum and dad threw the best events, they were always held in hotels across Glasgow, ballrooms filled with huge round tables. We would always dress up for the occasion; it was how we met Tilly and Paddy in the first place. Damian and Paddy were a similar age and had a lot in common, they were both passionate about cars and boxing and that was the main thing that made them click.

Tilly and I were almost twins, we liked the same movies, music, and we followed the same celebrities on instagram, we both had long dark hair and petite frames. Tilly felt like a younger wealthier little sister, she always got what she wanted. She wanted hair like me – poof it happened, an Audi TT for her twenty first birthday – poof it happened. She and I were like two peas in a pod, only difference, I worked for my lifestyle and she had it on a plate #jealousmuch. She was a sweet girl so it wasn't as bad as it sounds. When we arrived we were greeted by Tlly's parents. Her mum dressed in a long black chiffon dress she looked absolutely amazing, she had been training with a new personal trainer and eating properly for the last few months and it definitely showed, she sparkled through the hallway welcoming everyone and hostessing their latest charity event. I loved how much effort they put back into the kids and funding for their football team, we were happy to be a part of it too, it was always a good night out and helped with our networking.

"Babe? Where are Paddy and Tilly?" Damian said ordering me a drink at the bar?

"Gorgeeeoouusssss!! How are you???" Tilly screamed from the other side of the room.

OH MY GOD!!!! Tilly looked incredible. She strutted towards us in a black herve leger style short bandage dress. Jeez, head to toe she was perfect her makeup was flawless.

"Oh my god! I am so happy to see you guys!" she said squeezing me. "Do you notice anything different?" She said twirling around in front of me. Different? Is it maybe that you look like you're going to a movie premier instead of a charity event in Glasgow? Is that what it was?

"I'm not sure babes, but you look absolutely amazing."

"Well. . . I got my boobs done!" She said smirking.

"What? You got your boobs done? You're twenty-one? I mean you look amazing for it, but did you really think you needed them done? I never ever noticed that you needed it"

"Paddy loves them!"

Of course, he does, he's a man, I remember I wanted to get my boobs done once but I was far too scared to go under the knife. I don't ever remember her boobs, even when we are the boot camp I genuinely never noticed. I suppose if she felt bad about it then I'm happy for her, but honestly she looked amazing.

"No wonder, you honestly look stunning!"

"No way babe, it's just something I wanted to do to make myself feel better, enough about me you look beaut as always!"

Euan and Emily were late as usual. "Hi Dolly, sorry Euan took ages coming home from work," she said kissing me.

"Hey Shorty! How's the new job going?" Euan said patting my head.

"All good actually, I really like it. The people are so nice."

Emily and I ran off to the bathroom for a quick pow wow.

"What's with the chebs? Could she get any better a push up bra?" Emily snorted.

"Babe, it's a boob job." I sniggered, Emily is so funny.

"A boob job? Come on, what the actual? She's twenty friggen one!! Is she desperate or what?"

"Em, I understand what you're saying but it was her decision and she does suit it."

"Yes dolly I know. I picked Euan's jaw off the ground for him. Arsehole." She giggled.

Was it really an act of desperation to get a boob job? Or if you did something to make yourself feel better does that mean everyone has to have an opinion behind your back? I suppose no matter what you do everyone will have an opinion one way or another.

When we got back to the table, Paddy as usual ordered us too many shots and before we knew it the boys were smashed. Tilly, Emily and I took over on hundred photos hoping for good enough pictures for Facebook and instagram. Vegas would be so much fun with us all together, although someone would potentially need to carry me or David home if we had drank even half of the shots the boys have taken tonight. I couldn't wait until tomorrow, Damian and I have got the weekend off and we are going to look at our new house!!

Chapter 12

The truth was I loved our house; it was small and compact but at the same time had heaps of space. The ceilings were high and the hallway was long. We were lucky enough to have the massive wardrobe in the hallway with a ten-foot height, between two of us we had too many clothes. We had shelves and rails, shoe racks for me and tie racks for Damian, it was so us. The house was crisp white and everything we had was new. We took our time on decisions and made sure that when we did get what we wanted it was perfect. We'd waited so many months for the sofa; and by the time we got it we were so used to sitting on the floor that we continued to sit there, just in case we damaged the new sofa of course.

We decided to look at our dream sandstone house; it was a week before Vegas. But we were ready for another challenge, to build something new together. It was only a matter of finding the right place; this property was less than five minutes away from our current home. It was the first house on the left-hand side of the street, the exact same house number as my mum's number one – some would say it was a sign. It was three stories and had a beautiful beige sandstone color outside, the house currently had a red door but we would definitely paint it black. The lady that owned it had been moved to a nursing home and the family decided it was time to sell. As soon as we opened the door I had a vision, a shiny black banister with cream carpet flowing down the stairs, it would be minimal and elegant, it would be like a dream coming to life.

"It smells a little bit damp baby!" Damian whispered so the man wandering around with us couldn't hear. "We could maybe get a little deal on this place."

I'll never forget when we looked for our first place; every property we looked at Damian hit his head on the light fixtures as soon as you walked into the any property. Being 6 ft 4" did have its draw backs. However this place had more than enough head space, probably enough for one Damian to stand one top of the other. It was so bright and airy, and there were so many rooms. How would we fill it?

"Gabs! Look at this?" Damian took me by the hand down stairs to the basement; there were two large empty rooms and a door leading out to the back garden. "We could make the first room a massive walk in wardrobe with the island in the middle? And then walk through to like a dark and cozy spa bathroom? What do you think?" he asked.

"What color?" I questioned.

"It'll need to be black and white for the wardrobe and greys for the bathroom. That garden is a mess, and let's be serious we don't have time to be garden people. We'll need to deck that all out and get some astro turf for Penny?" His enthusiasm stunned me. "We would make a good house though, I just don't know about this street. I mean its close and everything for work, the dog, the area we like. I'm just not sure. Although I can imagine how everything would be."

"Rather than rush then, why don't we go to Vegas and when we come back put the house up for sale. Once it sells we can look at options. Plus we can always live at my mum's for a bit."

This year was only going to get better, before we know it, it would be Christmas and if all goes to plan, we can squeeze in another trip to Dubai and then we'll be hosting Christmas dinner in our new house. Our perfect dream was finally falling into place.

Chapter 13

"Babe, I'm gonna g to Stirling for the car show tonight with the boys." Damian was shuffling around in the kitchen with a protein shake.

"Ok, I'm going to town to get some new makeup after work, I'll just have dinner with my mum and see you when your back."

Glasgow in the evening was cold and grey, House of Fraser was bursting with people, and they had just announced their summer sale. This was all I needed, to buy even more unnecessary items I don't need right before this holiday. Think Gabriella, Foundation, powder, mascara and an eye liner. It's not that hard; just don't look at anything else; if you don't look at it it's technically not there. The stands sparkled around me and I was being sucked in by the beautiful people urging me to shop more. An hour or so later I was leaving, full of bags. Foundation – check, eyeliner – check, mascara- check, powder – check, new pair of jeans – shouldn't have done that, dress for holiday – ok I can justify this, Shoes for work – always required, new passport cover and luggage tag – well I've done it now. It was dark walking back to the car. Glasgow sometimes had an eerie feeling about it, ok I'm being dramatic I was scared of the dark and walking up a multi-story car park on my own, who wouldn't feel scared?

"Damian, hey the shops were crazy busy. I'm just walking back to the car and I wanted to say hi, I didn't want t-"

"Gabs! What the fuck is it!! I'm out with the boys, I only left an hour ago, why are you such a fucking psycho!!!!"

"Damian, that wasn't it at all. I just wanted to say hi because I was walking on my own, it's pitch black. I didn't realize. . ."

"Gabby, just go away." And he hung up.

What the hell have I actually done that constitutes that type of answer? I only wanted to say hi because it was dark. It wasn't even 9pm he doesn't even normally leave until then. Whatever if he wants to have boy's night, he can have boy's night. Stupid car show, no-one even cares about that in the first place. I can't wait to have my dinner and a glass of wine and get home into bed, I needed to shake off this Damian stress he's being such an idiot these days, it's like he picks and chooses when he appreciates me.

A little after ten o'clock I got home and started hiding my newly purchased goods. Making Damian's bad mood worse is not a good idea.

G: babe, what time are you due home? Penny and I are going to bed soon. X

Half an hour later.

Damian: be home about 11pm; just get yourself into bed xx

G: Ok Mr, good night. X

I could sneak one more episode of Kardashians on before I get into bed. A little fix to cheer me up, the better spirits I was in would make his little tantrum go away much easier, I mean it's not a big deal; I only phoned to say hi.

Once the program finished Penny and I were ready for bed. Penny was acting strange she sat on Damian's side of the bed staring at the hallway towards the front door.

"Penny baby, come and see mummy and get some sleep?"

She sat staring straight ahead at the front door, weird dog. I drifted off within five minutes, too tired to dramatize Penny's awkwardness.

A few hours later I jumped out of my sleep, where was Damian? It was one thirty am. Shit had something happened? His line is ringing out, I tried again no response. Shit.

"Euan, I am so sorry to call you so early but Damian went to the car show and he hasn't come home and I don't know what's going on. . ."

"Euan? Who is that?" Emily yawned in the background.

"Darling, he's at the car show with his friends just relax."

"It's one fucking thirty am, it finishes at ten thirty!!!"

"Gabby! Don't yell at me, maybe they went for some food, just chill."

Chill? He actually wanted me to chill. It's a Thursday night and Damian is at the "car show" which finished hours ago and he isn't home. What if there has been an accident, what if something happened to them? I'm not fucking crazy.

"Ok Euan, you're right I'm sorry I just panicked. I'll call you tomorrow.

Good night, and say good night to Emily I didn't mean to wake you up."
"Good night pal."

Who did Damian think he was not even calling, he said he'd be home at eleven, it's nearly two am. We've got work tomorrow.

"Damian, GOD! Are you ok? Where are you?"

'Gabby! Stop being such a fucking retard. We met my cousins and were just having a catch up. Be normal and go to bed I'll be home later."

"How much later?"

"Later Gabs. I'll see you in the morning."

He'll see me in the morning? Really? Who did he actually think he was? Should go to my mums and see how much of a fright he gets when he returns to an empty house. How could he treat me like this? I haven't asked anything abnormal. I am so angry, penny lay on my chest as I tried to calm myself down. What the hell is so important at two am he has to see his cousins at this time anyway, He's acting so out of character.

The front door opened quietly and Damian came into the bedroom.

"G, calm down man. You're acting like such a psycho today."

I was not speaking to him. Not a chance, how dare he treat me like this, I lay facing the window hoping he thought I was sleeping.

"G!" he cuddled me.

"Damian, seriously get away from me, what are you playing at? I do not want to speak to you. I need you to leave me alone. I'm going to sleep."

"Ok babe, good night, I didn't mean to do that to you, I only sat talking to my cousins."

I may come across like a fool but I know when my gut is telling me something isn't right I know it isn't right. I hope he's not getting involved with dealing drugs. There's no way this is normal Damian behaviour, either way I'm removing myself from the situation. I have way too much to think about without worrying about Damain and his extracurricular activities. If He's not dealing drugs; he's just being a selfish bastard like every other man on the planet. Get to sleep Gabriella, you have work tomorrow.

Chapter 14

It was almost time for our pre Vegas Hangover party, basically the theme was "The Hangover" – the idea is we would all drink ridiculous amounts of alcohol and have terrible hangovers the next day and hopefully not get into as much trouble as they did in the movie. I had a "drug dealing monkey" in the corner selling haribo sweeties, a cocktail bar set up in the kitchen, champagne fountain and enough snacks to feed twenty people. This was the beginning of our holiday, we only had a couple of weeks left and we would not have the opportunity to spend any more time together as a group until the actual holiday now. I couldn't get Emily and Sophia off the phone or whatsapp but Tilly had went quiet, she'd hardly spoke in the group chat since Sophia's birthday and I haven't spoken to her once. She'd been to the shops with Sophia but other than that it was radio silence, I hope she is ok, maybe she was embarrassed, I hadn't heard from her since Sophia's birthday, but everyone goes through phases of drinking to much and being silly it was normal to do that in your early twenties, at least we could spend some time together tonight. I'm sure it will all be ok.

It was standard practice for Euan and Emily to arrive first and like always Emily and I "pretended to get ready in the makeup room" so we could chat.

"Babe, did you hear Tilly and Paddy broke up? Like for good?"

"What? No surely not, when did this happen?"

"Maybe three weeks ago?" Emily whispered, three weeks ago? She's not been speaking to me for that long, maybe this was the issue?

"Well I haven't actually spoke to her for weeks. I assume this is what's wrong. Maybe she doesn't know how to say she's not coming?"

"I hope she doesn't come!" Emily chuckled. "Ok, I'm not that mean she's ok, she just got under my nose about with the boobs and the whole hanging on Euan thing."

"That's understandable, but do you really think it will work three proper couples going to Vegas together and one 'broken up' couple coming with us?"

"I told you they'd ruin the ambience Gabs."

"I'm sure they'll make back up there's no reason why they shouldn't."

Shortly after Sophia, David, Tilly and Paddy arrived, and before we knew it the drug dealing monkey was out of Haribo and the Champagne fountain was dry. Sophia pranced around the living room showcasing her latest dance moves as David made a terrible attempt to copy her, Paddy cheered them on with a finger pointing rave move, whilst Emily and I giggled at them in the corner. Euan and Damian were entertained in the kitchen by Tilly, surprise surprise.

"Babe, can you come to the bathroom with me."Tilly said pulling my arm down the hallway.

"yeah of course, are you ok? I feel like we haven't spoke."

She looked at me awkwardly, "Yes of course I just feel a bit uncomfortable, the whole Paddy thing. It's sort of become very final."

"Are you sure you guys can't work it out?"

"No babe, I'm done he's not the guy for me, I heard he took drugs at my birthday last year and he just doesn't treat me the way I want to be treated."

"Aww babe, I'm so sorry to hear that I hope your ok?" What the hell was she talking about, he just paid for her holiday to Vegas? And bought her loboutins for her Easter present for god sake. What more could he possibly want, he was good looking, loyal and made a lot of money which he never minded spending on her. I'd literally die if Damian paid for a holiday for me.

"I'll be fine babe, I hope it just doesn't make it awkward if we come separately, I'm going to get a separate room."

A what? A separate room? I hope she doesn't think this is a single's holiday, it'll be way awkward if we need to wingman her when were out at night. Damian would kill me if he knew I was even close to that situation, this isn't going to work.

"whatever you are most comfortable with hun, but if you want to cancel don't worry we won't hate you for it."

"Cancel? No way I can't miss this, I am dying to go. I'm even on those tablets for my skin you know roaccutane? They said I shouldn't go out in the strong sunlight but I just can't miss this."

"Babe, don't do anything that will damage your skin, in the long term it's not worth it."

"I'll be fine, come on let's go back through to see everyone."

As we walked back through to the chaos that filled my living room I was in shock. Is she really that desperate to go to Las Vegas that she'd number one book another room to be away from Paddy and two, risk her face to be there. I mean I am excited to go but is it normal to be that excited? Maybe I've forgotten what it's like to be twenty one and ready to explore the world? Who knows? As soon as I sat down David picked me up and spun me into some sort of strictly come dancing move, we span around the living room twirling and dancing as Emily and Sophia cheered us on.

"GET THE FUCK OFF ME!"

"WHO THE HELL ARE YOU PUSHING!"

"Right! That's enough, Paddy! Euan! Get a grip!"

Damian dragged Paddy and Euan into the hallway as scrambled to punch each other. "They're not doing this in our house Gabs! SERIOUSLY YOU TWO GET A GRIP!", the scuffle continued down the hallways and out of the front door, Emily and Sophia followed everyone outside and here I was left in complete silence in the living room. Glasses and bottles left everywhere, empty sweet packets and crisps crushed into the floor. What was that about? It was best I cleared this up while I was in the mind too, if I wake up tomorrow and see this I'll have a heart attack. Around forty minutes later I sat down – where is everyone? Why has no one came back? I called Damian twice – his phone was in the kitchen. Euan nor Sophia answered, I wonder if the police had lifted them for fighting in the street. Why does Damian not ever think of me? He clearly hasn't had one thought about me? Maybe I should go downstairs and check on them, shit! He's took my key? Where is his key? After ten minutes of raiding drawers and pockets I couldn't find his key. I was literally stuck in the house with no idea where anyone was. Great party Gabby! Hi five you! You're about to go on holiday with a bunch of crazy people that leave you!

It was 2am, there was no point in staying awake, I was half drunk and working tomorrow. I couldn't wait up for everyone all night, I'm sure they could figure it out themselves. Eight hours later I woke blinded by the light coming through my window, I should've shut my blinds, god I feel sick, I need to remember not to mix drinks in Vegas.

"OH MY GOD! WHAT THE HELL ARE YOU DOING HERE!!!" I turned around and David was lying fully clothed sleeping on top of my bed beside me.

"Gabs! It's ok, Sophia told me to stay with you, everyone left and she knew you'd panic, she had to be home as she's teaching tomorrow. I just stayed because there was no key to lock the door and Damian wasn't home. . ."

"Damian wasn't what?" I stood up and began fixing the bed? Where is Tilly's car? Did she not park it out the car park last night?"

"Yeah Damian helped her move it, do you not remember?"

"remember what? There was a fight between Euan and Paddy, everyone left and I tidied up?"

"well yeah, pretty much."

"pretty much what? Where is Damian?"

"he's in the spare room?" In the spare room? Well why didn't he come in and sleep beside me?

"Are you ok?" I asked him.

"You disgust me!"

"Disgust you? What are you talking about?"

"I go out to break up a fight and I come back and you're in bed with your brother in law!"

"in bed with my- What? Are you mad? I stayed up when everyone left, tidied the whole house, called you? Waited and fell asleep. I woke up in bed under the covers in my pijamas and David was on top of the covers fully dressed! Don't make it sound like that!"

"It is what it is!"

"Do you know what I am done with this crap, don't even bother speaking to me!"

Chapter 15

I really need my hair done, Vegas is such a glamorous place, and right now I am so plain Jane. I just can't afford great lengths extensions, Krystal does hair? Maybe I should ask her, every girl needs long beautiful locks for Vegas.

G: Girlies !!! Guess who's booked her extensions!!!!!!!!!X

Sophia: don't tell me - you? Xxx

Emily: Can't to see it gorgeous!! Xxxxxx

Tilly: Oh did you? Which brand are you getting? I was thinking about getting mine done too but I didn't know which brand to get? Xx

G: I went for beauty works this time, I normally get great lengths but I'd rather save the money from them and some extra spending for VEEEEGGGAASSSS!!!!! X

Tilly: That sounds good, which length are you getting? Xx

G: I think I'm gonna go super long and get 20" hair this time. X

Tilly: oohh sounds fancy, I'll probably get mine done I just need to speak to my dad xx

Emily: pics pleaseeeeeeeeeeeeeeeee, when are you getting it done? Xxxxxxx

G: not till Friday, bye bye short boring hair, Glamorous Gabriella will be back!! X

Emily: Can't wait, my sisters friend is giving me a weave, Sophia please help me do my hair when we're there, I can't even use a pair of straighteners never mind with a weave too xx

Sophia: trading hair for makeup doll! There's no give without take!! ha haXxxx

G: So excited now girlies!!! X

Friday couldn't come quick enough; it was only a few days before we go to Vegas. I was nervous excited, panic is settling in and I just hope everyone would get on. Sophia and David better not be too much to handle, they can be a bit over powering at times.

Krystal's house was unbelievable; it was a beautiful sandstone house with black high gloss painted gates and pristine gardens at the front. Her fiancé John owned a building company and no expense was spared during the interior re styling of their stunning new house. The interior was like a palace, it was the perfect combination of modern traditional. Her taste was a mixture of classic black white and gold, with shades or crushed velvet and satin throws in her bedrooms. Damian decided he would come an hour or so after the appointment so he could have a beer with John and we can all have some food and a catch up before we go to Vegas.

By the time I reached the house it was nearly 8.30pm. Penny was with me and we sat in the back room whilst Krystal washed, dried and straightened my sad short locks. As she prepared the hair I patiently waited to be beautified, I forgot how amazing the feelings of long luscious locks were like. I hadn't had extensions for nearly a year and I immediately regretted not putting them back in before now. Operation beautiful Gabriella commenced.

"How's all babe? Is work good? What is the gossip with Tilly and Paddy by the way?" Krystal asked.

"Yeah, it's not bad honey, just looking forward to my holiday now. Gosh I know, well they decided to split up. Tilly said he's not the man for her anymore. I think he apparently took some cocaine at a party or something. She still wants them both to come and have separate rooms."

"What!! Is she insane? Why would you even bother still coming? It's so weird. You know what babe leave them to it don't get yourself stressed. What about you? have you got everything?"

"Yeah I know, I've ordered all my bikinis from Victoria's secret and they've all just arrived. I maybe just need a couple of last minute bits and pieces, that's it really?" I said.

"Hair is gonna be so fab beautiful, I am so glad you finally decided to get back to it, you need to be glam!" she said giggling, "What time is Damian coming around, John should be back by 9 and we can order a take away. What do you fancy?"

"He should be here by 9.30, so maybe a Chinese? I'd quite like a chicken curry." I replied. I'd better text Damian and remind him."

G: Hope you got home from work ok honey, I've got Penny and were gonna order a Chinese, what time will you be here and what do you want to eat?" X

Damian: I'm gonna go and see my mum while I am nearby so I'll get food there and I'll be with you before ten. X

"He's gonna have dinner at his mums, it's like five minutes from here and he'll be here by ten."

John brought in the Chinese and Krystal took a break from my hair. I needed 200 bonds, this would be a full on job for her on a Friday night. The well behaved guest that I am cleared everyone's plates and washed the dishes before going back to patiently wait for Krystal finish my hair.

Krystal was on a roll, and the more hair she put in the heavier it was on my back, it felt amazing.

"I'm not looking forward to drying these." I chuckled, "Can you just come with me and do my hair the whole time?"

"Babe, I would love to come, but work is has been so maniac, John and I are still saving for the wedding. Otherwise you wouldn't have a choice I would be there." She gushed. "Pass me another packet of hair John!"

"I know babe, but your wedding will be amazing." And amazing it would, everything Krystal did was the best of the best – she could give Kim Kardashian a run for her money, I can just imagine it will top Kim Ks or at least meet the standard. John and Krystal met less than two years ago and in whirlwind designed their dream home and are engaged to be married.

Damian and I were more laid back, we had a beautiful apartment, it was small but it was perfect us and Penny. We'd looked at our dream sandstone house last week and hopefully we would finalize the details and begin the re-modeling when we got home from Vegas. There was no rush for us to get married we were enjoying our lives and our holidays and I'm pretty sure if we do all that Damian will not be buying me a real engagement ring anytime soon.

It was 10.30 and no sign of Damian, inside I was worried but it was better to act normal. I didn't want to embarrass myself in front of them.

"Where is Damian Gabriella?" John asked, "I'll drink all these beers on my own otherwise."

Where was Damian that was a good question?

"I'll message him, he's probably been held up."

G: Hey babe, you nearly here? X

I put my phone down and focused on my hair. Twenty minutes passed and no reply, this whole no reply was becoming the norm.

"Tell Damian I have four beers left. So tough luck" said John.

"Babe, those pictures of you and Tilly on Facebook from last week are gorgeous, no wonder it's her profile picture, you both look amazing." Krystal gushed.

"Thank you babe, I know, if I could get away with someone else other than Damian being in my Facebook picture it would definitely be that one! I'm just gonna call him in case he hasn't seen his message, give me two seconds." I looked at Krystal and walked into the hallway closing the door behind me. His line rang out, rang out at 11pm on a Friday? This is the second time this has happened this week – No over thinking Gabriella, it's a coincidence. I walked back into the room smiling although my stomach was in knots. It was strange, if he was at his mums why number one would he still be there at 11pm on a Friday and two not answer his phone.

Damian always answers his phone. I tried to hide my look of concern in front of Krystal and John. Krystal carried on doing my hair and as we came to the last section it was nearly 11.20pm.

"I'm just gonna try him again doll, just in case something is up." I walked into the hallway again and called him.

Ring. . . ring… ring . ring. He didn't answer. I stood for a few seconds trying to control my nerves. Something is not right, why would he not answer the phone? Why would he not be here around the time he said? Damian is never late for anything? Never mind a night on the beers with John. It just didn't make sense, and then he called.

"Hey baby, is everything ok?"

"I was worried something had happened?" I said to him nervously.

"Is this a fucking joke? I'm at my mum's and I met my cousins. I don't need to check in for fuck sake!" He was fuming and I couldn't understand why. He said he'd be here and he hasn't showed up. Calling would be a normal thing to do?

"Em ok, well I just wanted to call because you said 9.30 then you said 10pm. John is asking where you are, and it just felt strange because you don't normally do this, I mean are you gonna come?" I felt sick, physically sick. Why was he acting like this it was so out of character?

"I'll come when I'm fucking ready!" he yelled.

"Ok, well I'm nearly done so I'll head home after this then." he hung up the phone and my heart sank. Since when did Damian become so cruel and nasty? Maybe I've done something wrong? I walked up the stairs to the bathroom and sat my head in the toilet I felt sick with nerves. I hated being sick, please don't be sick Gabby. I stood for a couple of seconds and nothing. I spat in the toilet and stood up, I washed my mouth out in the sink and brushed myself down so I could go back down stairs and face John and Krystal.

"Babe? All ok?" Krystal shouted upstairs.

"Yeah, I'm just coming down, Damian got held up at his mums, I just needed to go to the bathroom, Let's get this hair finished, shall we?" I said smiling walking down the stairs towards her.

"It'll only take fifteen minutes more." And Krystal continued finishing the remaining bonds at the front. She cut off the ends and swoosh I had beautiful long hair.

"Remember and take two painkillers before bed doll. It'll be a little uncomfortable the first few nights." Krystal took me into her fancy living room to take some pictures for Facebook.

When we returned Damian was in the back room with John. I paid Krystal and hugged them both goodbye and we walked down the large driveway to the cars. I have never felt like I didn't want to speak to Damian, but today was different I felt betrayed by him. He was always so upfront and honest, why would he wait till midnight to show up at Krystal's especially when he had no intention of actually coming in the first place.

"I'll meet you at the house." I said as I put Penny in the car. I didn't look at him directly but I waved to Krystal and John at the window.

"Babe, calm down, I seen my cousins and was catching up. They'd got new cars and stuff." Damian looked at me with soft eyes.

"Let's just drive home; I'll see you at the house." I played the music in my car loud to drown out my anxiety, why am I being so strange about this? We have been together for a long time, we know each other, we live together and we have plans together. He can go out and not have to check in every five minutes. Maybe it was me?

As we got home Damian started talking to me like nothing happened.

"Babe, my cousin got a new car, it's hardly the end of the world."

"That's fine and I get that but why did I feel so anxious about it? You're not acting normal. It's not right!" I put my pijamas on and brushed my teeth. I'd slipped into bed and turned the other way; I wasn't in the mood to hide how I was feeling. I gave it a good go in Krystal's but I am not doing it for Damian I didn't have the energy to put on a brave face. With tears in my eyes I fell asleep, but I needed to because I couldn't stand the thought of looking at him and hoping he didn't make me feel the way he did tonight.

Chapter 16

The next day in work I couldn't concentrate, I just couldn't put my finger on what was going on, first the cars show then Krystal's. It was so unlike him. He has to be having a mental breakdown, he was thirty two this year, and all of his friends were married and we were, well we were just us. I suppose probably in some lights we are quite selfish with our holidays and our jobs. Working six days a week was tough, we had limited time to see each other and just the pressure of being together for so long and not making that commitment was stronger than ever. But he did buy me this ring that surely meant something. To add more pressure to the situation I was learning a completely new type of customer and new method of selling, not to mention a completely different product. It was just getting too much to handle and we both needed a good holiday, we need to de stress and relax so we can go back to work and start achieving the success we changed jobs for in the first place. Nine hours of work had passed and Damian and I still hadn't spoken since last night, I started googling holidays to Dubai.

"wee yin, what you doing?" Scott asked. Scott was the newest person working in Porsche other than me; he was about ten years older than me and the funniest guy I had ever met. I never got a minute bar I was making coffees which were rated on an out of ten score card, or he would be over my shoulder reading my text messages and seeing what I was up to. I can't say I didn't appreciate it though; he made me feel like part of the family, he was the big brother I never had.

"What you up to wee yin?" Scott said munching a biscuit in my ear. "I know you're ignoring me"

"I'm just looking at Dubai, not sure about the whole Vegas thing anymore." I said nonchalantly.

"But Gabby? Why would you do that? You guys have saved and spoke about this for months. You have literally spoken about this for months. My ears are ringing with it? Are you mental?" he gasped.

"I just feel like something is wrong, Damian isn't himself and maybe he's having a breakdown. But Dubai is not for us it's just for me." I said staring at the hotels on the laptop.

"Wee yin!!" he said spinning my chair around. "This isn't normal. Why would you even think that? Or even want to go anywhere yourself? Just talk to him and sort it out." He looked at me as though I was crazy, I don't feel crazy I feel stressed and I need a break.

"Look I'm probably not gonna go, I just wanted to see my options and go from there. It's not a big deal."

"Ok, ok, it is a big deal if you're gonna do that though chick. If you go to Dubai on your own you and Damian are over, regardless if he's having a breakdown or not. Why not just wait and see what is going on before you make a rash decision."

No one actually understood where I was coming from, but I couldn't exactly say oh Damian didn't come home after the car show or the party or come to Krystal's when he said he would. But it's not like he was cheating on me or anything. He would never do something like that; he's just having a moment that happens to be affecting me. I held my silence but his reaction worried me. Why would we be over if I didn't go to Vegas?

I drove home to pick up Penny from my Gran's after work. I was deflated and sad, as I walked in the door I switched off my phone. Penny was in the garden playing with her ball, and my gran was watching her with a cup of tea with one ready for me too. Deep breath Gabriella, everything is ok. I sat in silence wondering what the best way to start my word vomit is.

"Gran, I don't know how to say this but I'm not in a good place." I held back my tears and took another breath, I hadn't said it out loud to anyone before but I was ready to crack. "Damian has been acting so strange recently and I just don't want to go to Vegas anymore. He's been acting so out of character and I don't want him to embarrass me or involve anyone in the group with his meltdown." She looked at me quietly and took in what I was saying. "Gran I just feel like if he doesn't know what he wants now when will he ever know? It's been nearly five years and we're looking at this new house and I'm just so scared it's not right. I mean were not even engaged, I just don't feel like I can wait anymore, if it's not happened in a year I think I'll need to call it a day.'

"Gabby do you not think maybe you're just stressing because he's stressing and that its worry that's creating all of these feelings? You've never wanted marriage and kids. That's why you have Penny is it not?"

She was right, but what if we get old and we don't have a family or anyone around us. I can't rely on Sophia to have kids that will love us, even though I know they would. "Everything is so out of sync, I feel like I'm drowning and no one can see it happening, I want to scream and no one is able to hear me. I looked at Dubai today and Scott says if I go it's over? But what could be over if we just take some space, I want to be able to breathe. I want Damian to be able to breathe; I just want this phase to be over. This isn't us at all. Were always on the same page and I just feel like we're going in two different directions. I feel like I don't know him anymore."

"Darling no one ever gets through life together without speed bumps. Your granddad and I had moments all the time. You need to ask yourself a question, do you love him? And can you see your life without him?" She waited patiently for my answer but I needed to take my time.

"Of course, my answer is yes. I don't want to have a day not speaking to him, but right now, I just can't understand this. And I don't want to live like this feeling under so much pressure, it's not like work pressure where I can get through it to the end result, this end result gives me a sick feeling and that's why I don't think we should go, but I don't know how to tell him. "
"Well petal, you need to figure out what is right for you. But no man is worth this level of pressure, he has to work through his thoughts and you need to decide how you can handle it better. You are a perfect couple and everyone knows that you will always be together, so dry your eyes and drink your tea. It's a blip."

She's right, I know she is but I feel flat. "Gran, I'm going to have an hour upstairs and hopefully that will make me feel better before I go home. Love you."

"Love you my girl." She said kissing me and I walked upstairs. Two hours later I woke up dazed, I need to go home. What time is it? Shit it was after eight. I switched on my phone and the messages poured through.

Where are you?

Why is your phone off?

Gabby is this a joke?

Seventeen missed call messages. It's only been four hours. I'll call him when I'm in the car.

"Thank you for putting up with me granny and watching Penny as always." I said picking her up and putting her things in the car. I called Damian as soon as I left the street.

"Where the fuck have you been!!!!!" Damian screamed. "Is this a joke?" he was raging and to begin with I couldn't even speak.

"I was picking up Penny of course; I switched my phone off for a bit."

"You switched your phone off? Really???? When do you ever switch your phone off? What were you actually doing Gabriella?"

Gabriella? Did he just use my full name? I just needed a break to process what has been going on, it's not a big deal. It's been a hard few weeks, how can he not see that.

"I just needed some time." I stuttered.

"Time? Time for what?" he was still screaming and I couldn't focus on driving, I was getting a headache and I couldn't think of anything worse than going home to this.

"Damian, you need to calm down, I needed time to process the last few weeks. I don't have anyone to talk to and I just needed to speak to my gran and sort my head out."

"Sort your head out! You've lost the plot. What have you got to sort your head out for? You're exaggerating as usual!"

"Damian, please stop shouting, I haven't done anything wrong. I went to pick up Penny and stayed at my Gran's for a while. I needed to process how I feel and I had a little nap to make me feel better. I'm really struggling with how you've been the last few weeks it's so out of character and I'm so worried its affecting me personally too." Telling him at this point might not have been the best idea.

"So you want me to believe that you went to your Gran's for four hours after work when I finish later than you? So you could process your feelings about me? You know that sounds like a complete lie! I don't know where you even get these ideas from its completely ridiculous!"

I couldn't shout or talk back, it did sound strange. I rushed home every night to be home before him. To make sure I had sorted dinner or poured him a beer. I can't imagine the shock on his face when he arrived home and we weren't there never mind my phone being switched off.

"Damian, I'm sorry. I won't do it again, I just feel under pressure. I'm in the car park I'll be upstairs in a minute, see you soon. Love you."

I don't have the energy to fight; we were going to Vegas in four days. I still had to pack and tie everything up at work as well as arrange Penny, none of us needed this, and it was becoming dramatic for no reason. He was screaming and shouting and I'm confused. Four days, it's only four days away. We'll need figure something out, I can't go like this.

Chapter 17

Today is the day we go to VEEEGGGGAAASSSSSS!!!
Damian and I woke up early and I packed Penny's things so she could go
and and stay with Damian's parents Christine and Damian Senior. Penny
loved his Gran's house; he was always so spoiled by them. We had a few
last-minute things to do today before Euan and Emily picked us up to head
to Manchester tonight, but hopefully the day would be stress free and we
could enjoy the first day of our well-earned holiday.

Christine was a warm and lovely person; she had so much love and care for
Damian and in all honesty for me also. She made me feel at home, and I
loved talking to her, although Damian and I weren't yet engaged Christine
and Damian Senior were family to me, and technically Penny was our baby,
so it was like taking the grandchild to stay with the grandparents.

"Are you excited to go darling" Christine asked.

"Yeah I can't wait now; I just want to get into the sunshine." Damian
squeezed my neck and I could see the excitement in his face.

"Now I know what you too are like but if you decide to you know . . . make
anything more serious when you're there can you at least call us? I've
already said to the girls in work that I wouldn't be surprised by you two!"
Christine winked at me.

God I hope she was joking my mum would kill me if we got married
without the family there. I never saw myself getting married away from
home without family there. It might not be such a bad idea though, get
married no fuss or stress and come home and get everything in place for
the new house. I couldn't help but dream about our beautiful sandstone
house with a Damian and Gabriella twist on Krystal's style. We'd have lots
of white linen with grey accents around. It would definitely be a dream
house and although we had no plans to have kids anytime soon I know that
having more space would just make life a lot easier should that happen.
Damian's idea to turn the basement into a huge walk in wardrobe with spa
feel bathroom/dressing room would be amazing. I was so excited to start
this next chapter with him. Vegas is the perfect trip to move to that next
phase, the last few weeks were a blip. Just like my gran said, we were
continuing on our forever.

Damian dropped me at the salon in Bothwell Main Street and I mentally
prepared myself for my waxing, I hated waxing, it was unnecessarily painful,

and didn't always give you the right result. But there was so much pressure to be Vegas perfect I was pulling out the stops, no pain, no gain.
"OK baby, I'm going to get my hair cut and I'll pick you up when I'm done." Damian kissed me and drove off.

"Well hello gorgeous, tomorrow is the big day I hear." Bianca was my beautician, I had known here for nearly twenty years. She was stunning, dark hair, tanned and curvy in all the right places. Bianca knew everyone and everything. I had done my work experience with Bianca ten years before and I will never forget that I hoped to be as successful as her. At that time she had a brand new Audi TT cabriolet and everything she owned was designer. She had her own business and her life was completely in her control.

"Tilly and her mum were here yesterday, she got her waxing and her nails done too. You will all have a ball, Jesus how much weight have you lost Gabriella? Is this all for Vegas?" Bianca loved a good girly gossip.

"I tried to lose a little, but it'll do. Yeah, she said she was coming in; everyone is pretty much ready to go. Did I tell you Sophia is dancing in the commonwealth games opening tonight with Rod Stewart?"

"Shut up!! Is she? She is an amazing dancer; I'll need to watch it! And How's that gorgeous big man of yours?"

"He's really good just getting his hair cut then he'll come and get me, we're gonna pop into town and pick up some last few bits and pieces and then home to finish packing and we'll drive down to Manchester with Euan and Emily." Bianca had an amazing way of making you feel completely comfortable even though I was in the worst pain and position of my life. She finished the waxing within twenty minutes thankfully. If it took any longer I would probably cry.

"I meant to say thank you for recommending Me to Tilly and her mum, they're never out of here, and they've become really good clients." I was glad because Bothwell was a small town and I liked to see people doing well. Not that Bianca needed my help; she was the best of the best.

"No problem, they're such a lovely family and Tilly has blended in well with the group, I'd probably be able to say were best friends now. We're going to do another boot camp together in a few months; the last one we went to was brilliant. You know Lucy from TOWIE, we did that one, although we went a run to the petrol station and bought a tonne of sweets. Ha ha we were starving."

"Fantastic darling. Well that's you all finished. If you need anything else please give me a phone and I'll get you booked in."

Damian arrived right on time; I loved it when he got his hair cut, he looked so much slicker. Damian was a perfectionist and meticulous with his appearance he looked so fresh and the smile on his face today was better than ever. With the last few weeks swept under the carpet we were finally going to enjoy our holiday.

"Ready to go gorgeous?" he said holding my hand in car.

'Always" I said laughing, although the last few weeks had been a bit strange and certainly things hadn't been perfect, this was us and there's no way anything would get in between that. People always made jokes about us being together, we were the David and Victoria Beckham of Glasgow, the OK magazine couple and the rest, and we had the white picket fence life. We didn't have millions in the bank or have smooth sailing lives. We both lost our grandfathers; we both went through the notions and stress of car sales, moving jobs, the highs and lows of life in general. But we were us, and I just wanted to make every memory together. Vegas is a place that I loved and that I always spoke of with Damian. A bit like Dubai I was obsessed, I couldn't wait for him to see it. Just like my gran and granddad we were going to see the world together and when the time was right we were finally ready, we'd have our three boys I'd dreamed about towering over me, just like their dad.

We laughed and joked the whole way to town, "you are so beautiful . . . to me, you are so beautiful." Damian sang in my ear as we made our way to Frasers. He needed a Ralph Lauren shirt for Vegas. I had a couple of my vouchers left from my Porsche winnings so I thought a wee treat wouldn't go a miss just in time for holiday.

"Babe, honestly don't you worry keep them for you." Damian said holding two identical shirts with a different coloured horse on the pocket.

"It doesn't make a difference whether we spend them on you or me, I've got everything, and so don't you worry. Why don't you just get both and then you have a choice?" I said.

"Ok baby, thank you. I love you." I still tingled every time he said it.

"Love you too." I smiled as I paid for the shirts and headed to the car. I was so hungry now.

"Shall we go back to the flat and ditch the car? Go to Bothwell and have a late lunch and a couple of glasses of wine? We are technically on holiday?"
"That sound's absolutely perfect babe."

The sky was crystal clear and the sun was shining. It was not hot by any means but we could sit outside and eat, it would definitely give us that holiday feeling. We bumped into Melissa and Michael. Melissa was an old friend of Damian's who he used to work with a few years ago. They had become very close couple friends of ours although they were a little older than me; we all got on like a house on fire. Melissa ran her dad's business and Michael was in IT. We spent most weekends with them drinking in Bothwell and having homeland tea parties on a Sunday. After eating lasagna and three white wines I needed a nap. I was never going to make it to Manchester alive if I kept drinking.

"Shall we head home babe?" I asked Damian smiling and giggling with the wine.

"She's ready to go Damo. Get that girlie to Vegas!!! And you two don't bother getting married without us there please!!!" Melissa said gulping her wine.

"Leave them alone Melissa, poor guy will have a heart attack with the pressure." Michael looked at Damian reassuringly. "They're pretty much married anyways, what's a bit of paper?"

"Right gorgeous, let's get out of here." Damian said scooping me up over his shoulder.

"Damian!!! Put me down!" I yelled. "We still have to pay." I was laughing uncontrollably. He's so embarrassing sometimes.

"Babe, I've left my wallet in the house. Can I transfer you?" he said worried.

"Don't be daft." I said putting my card in the machine. "You can make up for it in Vegas!"

I fell asleep on the couch as soon as we got home, only to be woken up by Damian as the commonwealth was starting and Sophia would be gracing our TV screens shortly. Damian had pulled the two suitcases into the hallway and left my travelling to Manchester clothes on the bed in the spare room. "Do you want a cuppa?" he was being super sweet and I couldn't help but being drawn in by it.

"Yes please babe." I replied. I was buzzing with excitement. I just wanted to get there now.

Sophia lit up the stage; she was phenomenal dancing beside Sir Rod Stewart. What an achievement, my sister was incredible, I was literally beaming with pride.

"Babe, I'm gonna take the bins out and I've asked Michael upstairs to bring it in tomorrow once they've been cleared."

"Good thinking batman," I said. "You excited now?"

"I can't fucking wait darling." he kissed me and walked down stairs with the bins.

I started reading my holiday book as to be honest I wasn't going to get much reading done in Vegas. It was going to be a completely different holiday than Damian and I had before. No relaxing and chilling. Partying and exploring, I couldn't wait, as I sat engrossed in the book I realized, he's been away for bloody ages. I looked out of the window and couldn't see him. Hmm, give him five. I went back to the book. I was the type of person when I read I forgot everything else existed. I read three chapters and realized it had been forty minutes. I tried calling his phone but it was switched off. That was Strange, I looked out the window but he still wasn't there. I wonder if he'd bumped into one of the neighbours and was standing having a chat in the hallway.

I opened the front door and began walking down the stairs. I hadn't even got down two stairs before I heard him coming through the bottom door. "Eh, What the fuck are you doing!" Damian yelled angrily walking up the flight of stairs below me.

"What? Is this a joke, you took out the bins and you've been gone for forty minutes!" He was clearly on something if he thought he could speak to me like that.

"You don't need to fucking follow me everywhere you know! I went and took out the bins and I was on the phone to Brandon." His face was red and he was raging.

"Why wouldn't you talk to Brandon in the house? What is going on?" my heart sank as Damian became this aggressive monster he seems to like being these days.

I had to walk away from him. I went into the spare room and put on my clothes for travelling. I felt physically sick the exact same feeling I had when I was at Krystal's. I just didn't like this feeling or this situation. Something is so wrong and I know it. But what am I missing? We've had such an amazing day.

I walked back into the living room and he was texting furiously on his phone. I sat on the floor opposite him.

"Damian I. . . I don't think we should go." I said quietly. I couldn't look him in the eye. I was so scared to look at him I thought I would cry instantly. "I just don't feel right and something has been totally off these last few weeks. I think we should leave Vegas and go to Dubai. I have a bonus coming on Saturday and that would be more than enough spending money for Dubai. Or if you don't think that's a good idea we could go up north and rent a lodge and take Penny. It could be just the three of us? I think we need some time together and maybe being around friends isn't the right thing right now?" I was panic breathing and holding the tears behind my eyes.

"Why would you say that?" he asked.

"Because you keep shouting at me and making me feel like I've done something wrong and I just don't know what's wrong it's not like you."

And at that moment I couldn't fight it anymore the tears were rolling down my cheeks like a waterfall.

"Gabriella, stop crying, nothing is wrong. We don't need to go to Dubai or up north. Look we've planned this for six months." He paused for what felt like a lifetime. "We can't let everyone down." he said looking right in my eyes.

"Are you sure?' I sobbed. "Why are you acting like this?"

"I'm just stressed, once were on holiday we can both relax and it'll be ok. Euan and Emily will be here in twenty minutes. Go and fix your make up."

He walked into the kitchen as I sat on the floor.

We can't let everyone down. We can't let everyone down. We can't let everyone down. The words circled my brain. I couldn't make a scene and not go at the last minute. As if it wasn't bad enough with the Tilly and Paddy drama. If we pulled out would be ridiculous, it was our holiday. We organized it and it would be completely embarrassing as a couple. I slowly put my make up on and got dressed. We can't let everyone down. Right, of course we couldn't.

"Babe! Are you ready? They're down stairs!" Damian pointed to the window and Euan and Emily hung out of a minivan. A min van for the four of us! I had kept a bottle of prossecco and pink plastic cups for Emily and I to guzzle during the journey down. Damian took the suitcases down stairs and I locked the door.

"Damian, do you have your key?" I shouted after him.

"No I don't need it, keep one here and just take yours. It'll be fine." he said walking out the side door towards the van.

I can hold myself together, I can do this. Believe him Gabriella, every ounce of my being wanted to go to my mums and forget the whole holiday. The effort it was taking to stop myself shaking in front of everyone was more of a struggle than I anticipated. The prossecco would hopefully help calm me down, my stomach was in knots I got into the van and smiled. "I'm so excited guys!" I said with a forced smile and closed the door behind me.

David and Sophia would drive down early morning before the flight so Sophia could participate in the commonwealth. We all met at the airport as agreed early doors, Tilly and Paddy stayed together last night, so fingers crossed they can make up and get back together. Sophia, Emily and I were cute, comfortable and casual as discussed in the group. But when Tilly showed up she was in a cotton knee length body con dress, her boobs out on full force. I was pretty sure we all discussed a cute casual and comfortable dress code, but hey ho, if she's comfortable in it to travel in that for the flight then really who am I to judge?

"Emily, I feel like shit, I need to shop. Can we go to the Dior makeup before breakfast?"

"Sure dolly, what do you want?"

"A new highlighter I seen. It's proper sparkly and will be just enough glow once I'm tanned."

"Of course, babes I don't know how to ask but are you and Damian ok?" Here we go. "Yeah, were fine, we've just had a few challenging weeks. I think Damian is having a mini breakdown. But we'll be fine once were on holiday. Don't worry, we are now de stressed. We have you amazing people, no work, no puppy to stress about and an amazing holiday head of us."

"Good babe. I'm gonna get one of those too. Euan will kill me but sod it we're on holiday!"

We walked to Frankie and Benny's for breakfast and met the rest of the crowd. David and the boys had started drinking, the pre-holiday beer that has to happen before anyone in Britain goes on holiday. I ordered my breakfast and observed the excitement of everyone. Michael Buble played in the background as we scoffed our faces.

"Damian do you remember that time we were in One Devonshire and they played this album?"

"No I don't why?" he said eating his breakfast.

"Oh, I thought you would, it was played in almost every place we went to together for a year?"

"No sorry I don't remember." and he carried on eating.

Ouch, that one hurt. So today he doesn't remember that Michael Buble was played in every single place for the best part of a year of dating that was strange. Don't react it's a simple conversation – he doesn't remember so what.

Emily and Euan paid a little extra for their seats and were sitting in a different place from everyone else with a little extra leg room. So Tilly, Sophia and I sat together and the boys sat together for the flight. I have to enjoy this; I know it wasn't our usual type of holiday or even a normal circumstance. But I must enjoy myself. I was stopping nerves from showing everyone that I was shaking by hiding under the blanket on the plane. The only thing I could think of doing was to sleep as much of the journey as possible and save my energy for when we got there.

The desert heat hit you in the face like an oven and as soon as we stepped outside the airport, the madness began.

"Limo anyone?" David casually said, pulling dollars out of his pocket. "Hell yeah boy!" Euan screamed. We all jumped inside the black hummer limo giddy with excitement, "Shall we do a tour of Vegas before we go to the hotel?" Tilly asked, her face lit up as she stared at the Las Vegas strip in the distance.

"Hey man, you wanna stop at the liquor store on the way?" The driver shouted above the music.

"Sounds like a plan, baby shall we get some champagne for the room?" Damian said nuzzling my ear and grabbing my leg.

The airport was not far from the strip, and in the distance, you could make out the buildings Trump tower, Paris hotel, the Luxor pyramid, Bellagio, Venetian, The Wynn, they sparkled in the Vegas sunlight bringing a magic and excitement that none of us had ever felt before. We would finally be able to party and experience something different than we have ever done before.

The liquor store we arrived at felt like something out of a movie. Bottles stacked higher than anyone can reach, tacky dollar signs with prices marked all over dusty crates and Vegas memorabilia bottle openers and fridge magnets everywhere. Between eight of us we had eight litres of vodka, three liters of Jack Daniels, six bottles of champagne and five bottles of white wine. It was safe to say this holiday was going to be messy.

As we pulled up to the Aria hotel the boys got rowdier. They were jumping around, screaming and clinking the bottles we'd just picked up. Couple by couple we all checked in. "Right guys! Drop your bags upstairs and we'll meet you all at the pool" David was like a kid in a playground.

"Let's just wait until Paddy and Tilly are sorted and we can all head upstairs together." The mother in me had to make sure everyone was ok. Some of the boys headed to the bar and I waited back with Emily.

"NO! I WILL NOT ACCEPT THAT ROOM, THIS IS A COMPLETE JOKE!!! I HAVE REQUESTED A SEPARATE ROOM AS WE ARE NO LONGER TOGETHER!! WHY WOULD I WANT TO BE BESIDE HIM!!!"

"Tilly babe, what's going on?" Sophia said with her arm around her at the desk.

"HE LITERALLY MAKES MY SKIN CRAWL! I WANT MY OWN ROOM AS FAR AWAY FROM HIM AS HUMALY POSSIBLE!!!"

"Tilly hun, do you not think it would be a better idea to have a room next door to Paddy? at least if were home late he can make sure your safe?" This was so strange, what is the issue?

"I DON'T WANT HIM NEAR ME!"

"Tilly please, we just want to have a good holiday, let's not start on a negative. If it's that a big a deal just asks them to change it. But lower your voice it's not the end of the world." Jeez I wonder what he's done to her for her to be so upset. Maybe we shouldn't have invited them. If anything, we don't need any drama on top of Damian's issues.

'Did she sort it?" I whispered to Sophia.

"Yeah, but what the fuck is she on about? Fucking diva, listen sis, we gawn fuck some sheet uuuuuppppp in heeeaaaarrrrr, forget those idiot's!" She said putting her arm around me, "are you ok?"

"Yeah I'm alright just wanted to relax!"

"This is going to be the best holiday ever sistaaa."

"I know, so glad to finally be here."

"Finally sorted girls, I'm on a different part of the hotel but just call me whenever. I'll meet yous at the pool in half an hour." Tilly said strolling off, like a weight had been lifted off her shoulders.

"Someone looks happy?" Emily snarled. "Right Euan let's go! We've got the pool to get to."

The casino buzzed with excitement, slot machines dinging and cash flowing all around them. Pretty waitresses delivered drinks to people playing poker at the tables and there wasn't a clock in sight. There were no windows and no sign of any outdoor light. We all stared in amazement at the mixture of under and overdressed people. It was a place where anything goes, as we got into the escalator the smiles on everyone's faces was almost like a TV advert, we were almost too happy and too excited to finally be here.

Our room was humungous. Floor to ceiling windows electric blinds, a super super king-size bed, marble bathroom with a shower that would fit six people (only in Vegas). Damian put the champagne at the side of the TV. "How amazing is this place?' I couldn't help but giggle. Damian jumped onto our bed and we lay down together for a second.

"I love you Gabby, so much you wouldn't believe. I'm sorry for being all over the place. I just needed a holiday, we're gonna have an amazing time." He kissed me slow looking into my eyes. "I mean it. It's me and you, always."

Our first day had already begun; it was thirty-eight degrees. Daiquiris in hand we all headed down to the pool to begin the tanning process. The pool was bouncing with people drinking and dancing, there were stag and hen parties, couples, girl groups, families. It was an inconsistent mix of people but everyone had the same carefree, fun attitude.

The boys headed to the pool bar whilst we all went to look around. There were three pool areas, one of which was called liquid; luckily we girls could get in there free.

"Might as well take a look around?" Emily winked at us.

"You girls got any ID?" the host asked.

"Sure!" Sophia said holding out her passport, as we all gave our passports Tilly stayed behind.

"I left mine upstairs guys, I'm so sorry. Look I'll go sit with the boys you guys can go look around. Honestly its fine, enjoy. There are free drinks for you guys why not go ahead?" Tilly said as she sauntered off and we walked into the beach club.

The hostesses were stunning, the idea of not wearing make up at the pool all of sudden felt like not such a good one. We were given three glasses of champagne and sat at a table near the top near the dj booth. The music vibrated through the crowd and every person in the place was dancing. "This is like something out of a movie Soph. Thank you for agreeing to come with me. It means the world that we'll finally get to spend some time together with the other half's."

"We might not be in any way similar or compatible but were sisters, and it's about time we started sending some time together."

"aww you guys! How nice is this? We're all together forever and ever." Emily said cutely chinking our drinks together. "I can't believe were actually living like this!"

The hostesses took our pictures and filled up our drinks. It was the first time we ever felt like we were living a different life. We would go back to the rest of the group tipsy but ready to start the holiday the way we mean to go on.

We pouted and posed for pictures and sat in awe of the people around us. "We should really go back and get everyone? What do you think?"

As we walked back Tilly sat at the side of the pool and the boys were in awe. I didn't ever think she needed her boobs done, but she looked amazing. She sparkled with confidence and you could see Paddy staring at her. He loved her so much; we had to help them sort it out of this break they'd decided on.

"Babe, I can't help but feel jealous that Euan is staring at Tilly."

"Don't be daft; she's a pretty girl of course the boys are going to look. She's young and got the world at her feet why would she not be lapping the attention. I just wish I had her confidence."

There is no way in this earth that Euan would cheat on Emily. She was his world he was being a man staring at a good-looking girl. I wish Emily could see the way everyone sees him looking at her she would never worry again.

Chapter 18

Second night in Vegas, and what a night this will be, we were going to the Chippendales! Birthday night round two!! I was buzzing with excitement, skipping around the room getting ready.

"Why are you so happy about this? Do you not think it's weird that you're going to watch naked men dancing about, it's fucking disgusting if you ask me?" Damian was not a happy bunny.

"Don't be jealous." I said laughing and kissed him. "Like they would be anything on you, I don't know why I'm so excited. " I hadn't even seen anything like it before, but it was Vegas and I suppose it's one of those bucket list things, the boys would go to a strip club surely? After I finished my makeup we headed downstairs to meet the girls, they all girls looked amazing. I was literally skipping around; I loved this atmosphere it was so fun, it was totally different from when Damian and I went to Dubai.

"Right boys, I'm taking my sister for a lap dance from an oily man, enjoy your night and we'll catch up with you later." Sophia was buzzing, we were singing its raining men in the hotel lobby, it was the best second birthday night out I ever had and it hadn't even started yet.

We all went to Tilly's room as she was on a different side of the hotel; we needed to go to a different elevator to get to her so it was best to all go together. It still didn't make sense to me why she'd want to be so far from everyone. What had Paddy done to her that was so bad?

As soon as we walked into the room it smelled strongly of black currant and freesias.

"Babe! How amazing does your room smell?" Emily said sniffing the air.

"It's that new one, Giorgio Armani Si! My mum got me it for the holiday. I can't stop spraying it!"

"How clean and tidy is your room, now we know why you wanted your own space!" Sophia chuckled. "prossecco anyone?" she said pouring herself a large glass.

"Sure!" Tilly said, "Even my drawers are organized, look at this." And organized she was, everything was folded and laid out, colour coded and pristine perfect. Her underwear drawer was full of satin and lace la Perla and Victoria's secret, all brand new and beautiful.

"My mum took my underwear shopping when I got my boobs done? What do you think of these?"

"I think Paddy's heart is well and truly broken, that's what I think!" Tilly genuinely was so lucky, everything she ever wanted she blinked and she had it. Her mum and dad literally have given her the world. It was the type of life you dreamed of, it wasn't the normal reality of the young and free in Glasgow. We downed our drinks and headed to the hotel for the show, we had to enjoy this lifestyle while we had it.

The Rio hotel was just off the main strip, as we walked through the casino to the event there were show girls everywhere, feathers and glitter and tiny little outfits. Their bodies were perfect; we were all giddy with excitement. "I wonder what this is gonna be like girls, do you think it'll be cheesy?" I should've had dinner before I started drinking again. "Sophia I should eat something."

"Fuck that were here now, just enjoy it, it'll be brilliant!" Sophia had got us great seats; we were only a few rows from the front. Tilly and I stood by the chairs whilst Sophia and Emily ordered the drinks.

The show was unreal, they could sing, they could dance, they could rap, they had charisma and they were totally ripped. I really didn't expect it to be so well put together, they sang a song called let's get ridiculous, and we did get ridiculous I think I had nine or ten vodkas. I was struggling to stand. When the show ended we were invited onto the stage to get a picture with the cast. 'Soph, I want that one." I said pointing at the muscley dark haired one. In all my glory I was smashed, to the point that Sophia carried me onto the stage and physically planted me onto the guys lap. We genuinely couldn't stop laughing, Tilly, Emily and I sat prettily whilst Sophia lay across three of the guys centre stage. This was a picture we had to get and would never forget.

In the shop you literally could buy Chippendale everything. I had to get Penny a little jacket they were too adorable. The girls all bought garters and we posed for pictures on the walls covered in these hot men. I had to go home, "Sophia, I am smashed, let's head back, you guys can go out and I'll get to bed." I bounced into the taxi and we went back to the hotel.

"Gabby, take a power nap and come back out." Sophia said, "Emily is gonna go out with Euan on their own for a bit, and Paddy is already in his room. It might be the travelling catching up on us. So it's me Tilly, David and Damian, we'll just be down here at the bar." They sat and waited for the boys, but I felt sick, too much prossecco and too many vodka's I couldn't handle it, I had to go upstairs and sleep it off.

When I got to the room, I miraculously took my makeup off and brushed my teeth, and placed my Chippendales picture beside my bed and lay under the covers. What a night we had, I think that is one of the best shows I've ever seen. I slept like a log, I was so tired and this holiday so far was nonstop partying. I was a bit out of my depth in the partying game, I'm not the best drinker to be fair but I'm giving it a good go.

Bang the door bounced open at 7am. It was Damian; he was taking full advantage of being in Vegas. "Are you not shattered?" I asked him, he lay down beside me. "Those casinos are amazing, what a place this is. What's that beside your bed?" he looked over at the picture.

"Oh wait till you see it, it's amazing! We honestly had such a laugh, and it was a proper show, singing, dancing, rapping . . . it was such a good night. I just felt a bit drunk so came home to bed."

He studied the picture for a minute or so and then looked at me. "Are you taking the piss? I'm out with the boys whilst your sprawling yourself all over some naked guy? This is a fucking joke, how can you sit there smiling when that's what you're doing, I'd be surprised if you were even in here last night!" He was fuming.

"Damian, please tell me you're joking? Of course, I was here I was sleeping, and it's a picture for god sake. All the girls are in it, it's not like it's just me." Jeez this guy was something else. "Get some sleep you're just agitated and tired." He rolled over with his back to me and went to sleep. Twat, why be that jealous of a picture? Although I did have to admit the guy was amazing. But why was he being so hard on me? I didn't even buy the ticket.

Chapter 19

He hadn't come home again last night, my nerves were starting to get the better of me and between the over indulgence with alcohol mixed with the stress it was really telling on my face now. What have I done wrong? Why can't he see me? We had so many amazing things planned and he was excluding himself from all of it. Casinos are fun but why would you go and sit there yourself every night?

I didn't have time to stress, I had to make the most of the break and I was excited for today, today was Calvin Harris at Wet Republic, and being Scottish we obviously loved him. David had sorted us with the table right in front of the dj booth, This was going to be something else and he's not even bothering.

Sophie: G, you up? Literally soooooooooooooooooooo excited for today!!! Are you getting ready yet? What's Damian saying? Xx

I couldn't tell her he wasn't home yet, it was too embarrassing.

G: yeah I'm up, just getting in for a shower and get myself sorted; Damian is in bed lazy sod. Catch you down stairs in an hour? Or an hour and half? X

Sophie: yes sis!! See you soon hot stuff XXXXX

Rolling onto my side, I checked his whatsapp, last seen two hours ago. Should I call him? I mean I am here with him? What if something has happened? Oh god, I'd better call him what a bad girlfriend I am.

The line rang and rang. No answer. . .

Maybe he was with someone else? Surely not? Why would he do that, he's still sleeping with me? I mean would I let a random pull in Las Vegas ruin our five year relationship? I'd need to think about that on a clearer head, all I can taste is vodka and my head is foggy.

I dragged myself into the shower and took my time shaving my legs, if I wasn't perfect for Damian McLaughlin, I'd be perfect for Calvin Harris. I do have to admit, I have a major thing for Calvin, that Armani advert I mean wow. My head took me to another place thinking of the perfection that is Calvin who would be standing ten feet in front of me in a few hour's time.

As I was finishing my makeup Damian dragged himself into the hotel room, the constant smell of vodka was taking its toll on me but what was worse was the strong smell of Jack Daniels when he came back after his boozy night. This time I thought I am going to take a different approach. I walked over and kissed him, stroking his head lightly I said. "You have a good night babe? Everyone is so excited about today; do you want me to make you a cup of tea while you're in the shower?"

He grumbled and walked into the bathroom closing the door. What an arsehole! My hair is was in perfect curls and the extensions Krystal had done were looking great, id magically managed to make my dark circles of worry disappear and I was smiling, clearly he couldn't see me. It was probably the alcohol so I am not going to take any notice of it and I am going to have a fun day. I was really enjoying my time with David and Sophia strangely enough. They were fun and carefree and made everything seem normal. David was like a brother to me, although he did call me sister at every moment genuinely thought the world of the guy. Soph and he had their ups and downs and I tried not to get involved, but they were a good match in my opinion.

As he walked out of the shower I was standing with my black bikini with the straps tying round my no longer there waist and I had my wedges on, I was so ready to go and dance. He stopped and looked at me, he didn't say anything but he smiled with his eyes. I wish someone recorded this moment, because that was us. Sometimes we didn't need to speak and we just knew it was me and you. I walked over and gave him a kiss. "Right Mr, let's get you ready we've got a party to go too." He drank his tea and fixed his hair, and just like that normality resumed, those ten minutes walking to meet everyone were the best ten minutes we'd had in days. We laughed and joked and we were smitten again, it was like nothing was even wrong. I was giddy with excitement, walking through the casino on the way to the main foyer was buzzing. I couldn't take my eyes off the people playing Poker at 10am in the morning. It was magical, people screaming with excitement, stunning girls standing with old men drinking champagne. We clearly had it all wrong in the UK.

"yesssssssssss!!!! Here we! Here we! Here we fucking go!!!!!!" David was dancing about like a maniac, "are we all ready for this??????"

"I cannot wait mate!!" This was the first any of us had seen Paddy this excited, it was amazing.

"Wee pal, you look amazing!" Euan twirled me around and Emily grabbed me. "Wheet whew doll, the girls have brought their game faces today!"

Everyone did look amazing, and we were so ready for today. We had spoken about it for months. I can't believe Calvin Harris will be standing in front of me, I might actually die.

We walked through the streets of Vegas as MGM grand was literally ten minutes away from us. The lights, the atmosphere, everything was buzzing and alive. David, Euan and Paddy were racing at the front of the group, laughing, dancing and shoving each other like kids in the playground, Emily and Sophia were chatting away, pouting and posing and taking selfies. I was walking behind mesmerized by everything around me, the buildings, the people, and the stores. It truly was a playground for adults. Slowly walking behind me was Tilly and Damian, they had a good friendship, and her family was close with us, I was glad we had all came here together it was strengthening our friendship.

I turned around to see if they were far behind when I saw Tilly up in Damian's face, they were close. Like really close. Did I just see? I couldn't have? The sick feeling immediately came back.

"Emily, Sophia. . . I think I just seen Tilly kiss Damian. I know I sound ridiculous but it was proper weird? She was in his face?" I am 5ft 2 and he is 6ft 4, now she might have 4 inches on me but there is no way she wasn't in his face without a stretch and wouldn't be for no reason?

Emily snapped. "Nip it in the bud!" and stormed off across the main road. Nip it in the bud? Nip it in the bud? This has to be my mind playing tricks with me. Tilly wouldn't do that, she was one of my closest friends, and Damian god I am being psycho; he was ten years older than her he wouldn't do that, would he?

Tensions were high, and Damian came towards me. "What the fuck Gabby?" he seemed angry at me, although I hadn't even said anything and he didn't know what I had seen.

"Damian, I feel like I'm missing something? I just turned round and I saw Tilly in your face. . . I . . .I mean how can see even reach you and why would she? This is just all weird; and you're not being yourself the whole holiday. I'm just worried." The Vegas heat was burning down on us and the excitement for Calvin was put on hold. I did not want to stand in the street and have this conversation. I wanted to dance and to drink and for the love of my life to walk with me not with fucking Tilly. He was huffy and walked away with the boys.

We started to cross the road and Emily turned to me, "When I said nip it in the bud I meant her, not him." And she strutted across the road. Her? Why would I need to say to Tilly? Do I need to say? God I really hate confrontation this is horrible. My stomach was turning as I walked up beside her, she was walking alone behind everyone, and I felt really bad. "Babe, listen I really don't know what to say, but I felt really uncomfortable when you were walking with Damian there. I know you guys are friends but Damian is going through something just now and I'd just prefer if you let me handle it? Maybe it is a good time for you to re kindle things with Paddy?" I looked at her hoping she understood me, I hated bad words between friends.

"You clearly are messed up! You're so insecure! If Damian wants to talk to me I am going to talk to him, you girls have singled me out from the word go!" she screamed and made a huuuuuuggggeeee scene. We were walking across a main road on the Las Vegas strip, talk about humiliating.

"I don't think that's very fair of you to say, considering we invited you and Paddy to come to Vegas in the first place and we've been good friends for a while now. All I'm saying is maybe focus on your own issues and let me focus on mines." I was shaking again.

"You need to get a grip!" she said cheekily.

"A grip! A fucking grip! See you, you twisted cow!! We all know what you're doing and we can see clearly what is going on here. My suggestion is you don't bother coming and ruining our day and get the fuck out of my face before something else happens!!" Emily was livid. I had never seen her like this before, she was always so sweet and delicate, I had no idea what the hell she was talking about, I mean Tilly did come across as sneaky at times but she is only twenty one, and hasn't ever had a girls holiday never mind a group one.

"Sophia, let's go, me and you don't need a day like this!" Tilly squawked looking at Sophia. I had to start walking away the awkwardness was too much to bear.

"If you think for one second I am going anywhere with you, your wrong! Paddy you better take her and get her to fuck! We need to have a good day and were not going to if she's here!' Sophia grabbed my arm and pulled me across the road. What had just happened?

Euan, Damian and David were walking into the MGM hotel, whilst Sophia and Emily held my arms tightly. "We've got you dolly." Emily said pragmatically. "stupid bitch, there is a line and you crossed it with Euan a few weeks ago, whose turn is it next?"

"Damian?" I grabbed his arm. "I don't know what the hell is going on with you, or with her but we can't do this, we need to start a fresh and enjoy our holiday? This is me and you, and I love you so so much. Can we agree to wipe the slate and start again?" He held me tightly and kissed my head. "Of course we can."

It was a weird feeling, I couldn't really stand with him, as I didn't want to be near him but we needed to be on the same page. Not that that affected anything these days.

Walking into Wet Republic was amazing. It was massive and we were escorted by stunning waitresses to our table at the front, everyone was looking at us like who are they? David had done so well. There were beautiful people everywhere, I was mesmerized. We ordered the largest bottle of Vodka I have ever seen. Not that I was complaining it was the only thing I could manage to take without feeling sick. Emily, Sophia and I were taking pictures and posing with random American muscle men, they were such good craic. I loved that about David, he didn't even care, he was never jealous of Sophia talking to anyone it was only about banter. Euan however had a sulking face but was trying to play it cool, and Damian, well fuck knows, he'd disappeared to talk to some guys he'd seen from back home at the back of the crowd. I was not ruining my day because of it, we drank and danced and laughed waiting for the main event.

That moment when Calvin came on was electric. As soon as the music started playing it was gradually building up, I might be anyone, A lone fool out in the sun, your heartbeat of solid gold, I love you, you'll ever know . . . were under control! As soon as the beat kicked in the whole place went insane, it the smoke was coming out of dj booth and there were people all around us. Emily and Euan were jumping on the chairs, David was screaming the lyrics and Sophia was on the muscle mans shoulders. This was a video for face book. I couldn't believe I was here; it was even better than I imagined.

Song after song the event only got better. This was by far one of my best days ever. We were all a happy drunk and after he finished we all stumbled out towards a taxi. In the state we were in walking would've taken us hours. Although I don't think it would've mattered in Vegas.

Not that we had seen much of Damian he took his time with the boys from home, Sophia was trying to talk him into coming back to the hotel for drinks with us. She didn't manage to persuade him, but this was the third night and he's left me every other night so what's the difference, it was the holiday norm for me. We'd had the best day regardless!

I went back to Sophia and David's room where Sophia lay face down in the bed with all of her clothes and her shoes on. David looked at me. "Sistaa it is not bedtime yet! Let's go down stairs and get another drink" David was like a child, jumping around and joking twenty four seven. I was so glad they were here so I could forget about Damian's behaviour.

"Fuck it!" I said, "I need to wash my hair though, I am covered in vodka." David waited in the room for me for around forty five minutes whilst I sorted myself for going back to the casino.

"Gabz . . . I'm just leaving my passport here ok?" he shouted from the room. "Ok D! Right I'm ready let's go!" We both walked down to the casino, it was one am and the place was alive, the sound of the slot machines throwing money out at people, screams and bottles of champagne popping it was something else. David was in a dream, dancing and cheering people on as we walked to the whiskey bar.

"Em, hello sir, we would like two of your finest glasses of whiskey on the rocks please." He winked at me and laughed. "I'm a pro at this, sir this is my sistaaaaaa, isn't she the best. We've left my wife upstairs face down fully clothed drunk in her bed and we want to get drunk, can you help us?"

David was a crackpot at most times but there was no way I was going to lie in that hotel room myself whilst Damian continued his nightly meltdowns. "David I don't know why you ordered me whiskey I don't even like it. I'm a three glasses of wine and bed kind of girl." I sipped it anyways what was the point in sobering up.

"Gabriella, listen no one knows what's happening with Damian and we all know you are worried but honestly don't worry about a thing, I'll talk to him and find out where his heads at. He's been stressed at work and you know he doesn't handle it the way you do." He swigged his whiskey and started dancing with his hands in the air. Maybe there was something really wrong. The whiskey was strong, but it was hitting the spot. "Should we go and see if Soph is ok?" He started dancing across the carpet mid yawn. "Yup, let's go get her we are going oooooouuuutttt." David was going to his bed he was wasted, thirteen hours of drinking was more than enough for him.

When we got back to their room Sophia got up and put some fresh clothes after her power nap. "You want to go back out? Really? Ok then we'll go back out." She danced around and was full of life, David had took his turn and passed out on the bed.

"Why not, its 2am, what else is there to do at this time." After around one million lift selfie's we entered the casino. It was still buzzing and no sign of dying down anytime soon. "Let's get a Cosmo." I said walking towards the jazz bar. Sister time is what I needed, it had been a very long day, I was on my fourteenth hour of drinking and didn't want to stop.

"Gabby? What's actually going on? Are you alright?" Sophia looked at me right in my eyes, passing me my drink I took the first gulp, this was the first time I'd said it out loud. "Damian hasn't come home any night since we've been here" I began sobbing and spluttering. "Something is wrong Soph, really really wrong. I can feel it from my toes and I can't put my finger on it. I feel so helpless, everyone thinks were coming here to get married and I can't but help think it's the end. Have I done something wrong?"

"Babe, calm down, David and I had a little chat and maybe he just needs a blow out. He has been acting strange and if I had the insight into his mind and I could show you what is going on I really would." She finished her drink and battered the bar for another. "Excuse me! We need some more drinks pleaaaaaseee?" she flirted with the bar man and within a minute we had two more cosmos. Crying publicly was harder without sunglasses, I was a mess, I'd never drank as much as I had on this holiday but the adrenaline was soaking it up and I couldn't feel a thing.

"We love Damian babe, but you're falling apart, if I could do anything to help you I would" Sophia had tears in her eyes and hugged me. "Another drink boss!" she gestured the barman over. "This is a sex and the city moment, two sisters who have never been this close getting through a weird time in Las Vegas together. Cheers!" She chinked the glasses and downed it in one, what a girl she was, I might as well follow suit and downed mines. "Shall we get one more for the road?" She nodded excitedly. Two men at the bar moved over to us and asked why I'd been crying for the last hour, ha the humiliation, "to be honest she's actually one of the most amazing people in my life and she's getting screwed over by a man that can't handle her." Sophia stood like a superhero, "but were gonna get through it!" she grabbed my arm as the bill came.

"Well two beautiful girls like yourselves should never have to deal with that, no sweat ladies the bill is on us. "He signed it to his room and walked away. "We hope to see you two again."

"What the actual? Did that just happen?" I giggled whilst we walked back to the lift. "I need my bed, I wonder if he is even home?"

"If he isn't fuck him Gabs, he's not wasting our holiday!" She kissed me on my cheek and we walked to opposite ends of the hallway to our rooms. My stomach was in knots wondering if he was there or not.

I opened the door and the room was pitch black. "Damian? Honey you here?" there was silence, I switched on the light and he still wasn't home. It was 4am in Vegas and I was getting into bed alone again, I'm pretty sure this isn't what they say happens on TV.

Chapter 20

I lay for a couple of hours watching the door and wondering why he hadn't yet come back. It was so un-natural for him to act like that. Just as I was about to doze off my phone went, it was Paddy – Hey G , what's your room number, Damian has turned up at mine drunk and he can't remember where you live? X

Oh my god, he is such an idiot. I hope Paddy sees the funny side to this.

G: Hey Paddy, what's he like? We're 2206, thanks pal. X

Stupid idiot, honestly who even gets themselves in that state, around ten minutes later the door swung open, and the jack Daniels stench was back. He fell into bed beside me. "Damian, you do know what room number we are? That's not cool? Where have you been?" I looked at him hoping for a reasonable response. "I was in the casino, and I got drunk." He threw his money on the table although it looked like it was folded neatly the way he took it earlier on that day. "Damian!" I was starting to get pissed off with his behaviour, we were on holiday with our friends, and it was going too far. He started to snore, and I rolled onto my side, how could he be so selfish?

We slept for around six hours; but I refused to get out of bed before him. To be honest it was more my bed than his anyways. "I think you were out of order with Tilly yesterday, there was no need for you to treat her like that." He began making us tea and I huffed dragging myself to lean on the headboard. "Damian, I know I feel bad too, but more to the point I just can't get my head around you this whole time. You're acting like someone I have never met before; I'll talk to her today and sort it out from that side of things, I obviously don't want any bad feeling in the group, but you need to sort out whatever is going on with you. People are starting to notice."
We got dressed and headed down to the pool, my tan was really coming on now, and it was about time to be honest. Tilly hadn't showed up yet but I would make a conscious effort to talk to her and sort it out. At the end of the day she was the youngest and it didn't look right me attacking her like that with no valid reason, I wasn't that type of person but this weird feeling I had I couldn't shake, why did the girls act that way with her?

We were all sitting poolside drinking daiquiris when she arrived, she sat down near me. Sophia and Emily stood up to give us some space. The tension was obvious and I felt awkward.

"Tilly, I feel like I owe you an apology, I know you're not a bad person and I know it's not your fault whatever is going on. I don't want you to feel singled out or left out because you're not at all in any way. It just because we have never spent a lot of time together as a group before, and it may feel like you're being left behind that's really not the case. You and I are really similar and I would hate to lose our friendship over this, We have six days left and regardless of the tension or the horrible feeling I have I'd like to wipe the slate and move forward, is that possible?" I looked at her for a few seconds, and that horrible silence when you just don't know what was going to happen next felt like it lasted a lifetime. All I was hoping for was common ground and also that we would agree to enjoy the rest of our time and get on with it.

"To be honest, I think it's all been very unfair, I was singled out yesterday and it was all because of you!" she was aggressive and had major attitude. Save the situation Gabriella, be an adult.

"Tilly that was never my plan, I just didn't expect you and Damian to be so close, it made me feel very uncomfortable. I'm sure you'd be the same if anyone got close to Paddy."

"Whatever all you need to know is, I would never lie to you." She didn't look me in the eye she looked away with a bitchy attitude, the stupid bitch looked away. I grabbed her by the hair and held her head under the water while she struggled! How dare she do that to me!

Well I wish I had done that, in all honesty I didn't have the balls to do something like that so in true Gabriella form I smiled and held myself together.

"I know that babe; you'd have no reason to." I smiled sweetly and let her stand up and walk away. I wish I wish I wished I'd drowned her. There is no way that this is a normal situation, something is going on and I am going to get to the bottom of it.

Chapter 21

Damian huffed and puffed around the room, he was looking for something and I am not in the mood to help him right now. I sat on the bed drinking my tea looking at my chippendales picture, acting like I hadn't a care in the world.

"G, where the fuck is my cardholder!!!" he was impatient and angry.
"Your cardholder?" I asked.

"Yes my Louis Vuitton cardholder you got me for my birthday, where is it? You had it last!" he yelled.

"No babe, I gave it to you during Calvin, you said you wanted your money because you were standing with those guys from Hamilton." I replied. What an idiot, how dare he stay out all night drunk then blame me for losing his stuff. It should be me losing the rag at his behavior he's acting like an 18 year old on his first holiday.

"WELL ITS NOT FUCKING HERE IS IT!!!!!! SO YOU MUST HAVE IT!!!!!" he was not happy at all.

"Right! That's enough! You can't come home at 7am from being out at god knows where then accuse me of losing your card holder. You specifically asked for it at Calvin, so I gave you it. What about that guy you were with, what's his name? Bradley? Will he not have it? Or maybe you left it in the casino?" I don't know who the hell he thought he was talking to but I was in no way having this. He stormed around the room moving every single thing.

"Damian! Give it a break it's not there, you've lost it, just focus on thinking where you had it last."

"Message Bradley's Mrs. on Facebook, you have her on Facebook." Damian demanded.

"Damian, you lost it, you were out with him you message her!" I said throwing my phone at him and I needed five minutes of peace so I walked into the bathroom and got into the shower.

I don't know what I was going to do when we got home, but this is so out of character for him. My Damian didn't lose things, never mind not come home every night of the week. He was always charismatic and the joker of the group, he was the center of attention and for some reason here was nonexistent. David was constantly looking at him to join in with his crazy banter. It was sad actually, we were such close friends and family and to be honest everyone was starting to feel the impact of Damian's behavior. Damian was just as much of a brother to Sophia as I am a sister to David. The tension in the days were becoming unbearable for me, I am so embarrassed by his actions and his attitude towards everyone. I just hope they don't notice as much as I think they do. I'll put it down to stress and we can handle it when we go home, maybe he needs counseling - what a task it's going to be to get him to go to that. But not for couples there is absolutely no issue from my side. Only for himself, my shower lasted about twenty minutes longer than normal; I was so deep in thought, and bang! Damian was at the flung open the door.

"GOD SAKE ARE YOU NOT OUT YET!"

I had taken a while, but I genuinely have done nothing wrong. Were on holiday, there's no rush to go anywhere. Jeez you'd think I was the one acting out of character. I got out of the shower and he passed me the towel.

"Damian, you really need to calm down, we'll find it. It's not the end of the world. I'll give you my joint card and you can cancel your cards and use that for the rest of the holiday. It's not a big deal." I said.

"Whatever, it's just annoying, I was certain you had It." he said softly. "It's ok, just don't stress." I cuddled him and kissed his face. "I love you, even if you are an alcoholic bum."

"I love you too Gabriella." he said looking at me, his eyes were drunk and he looked so tired.

"Partying is getting the better of us. Maybe we're too old and should be sitting on the living room floor with Penny." I joked.

"I'd love that, I feel like that's what I need." he said.

We got ready without speaking to each other. MTV played on the TV in the background, I felt humbled by the silence between us. There was a strange tension, but I knew we would be ok. I just knew whatever was going on in his head we could work out. Or maybe Christine was right, maybe we were going to get married in Vegas and he can't handle the pressure to ask me. Mums always knew best, but could we get married under this pressure,

Sophia was obviously going to be my bridesmaid anyways but is this what was going on?

I pondered over the idea of a tacky Vegas wedding in a glittery mini dress alongside our closest friends, marrying the love of my life who never came home the whole holiday and stank of Jack Daniels. Hmmmm it didn't sound very Gabriella, but I do love him.

"Damian, Bradley's girlfriend messaged back, she's sent his number for you." weird why he didn't have it considering he spent a full day/night with them. "She said she hasn't heard from him for a day or so either. She's asking if you were with any girls?" please say no please say no.

"What? No of course not, we were just in the casino getting a few drinks at MGM." he replied.

Phew. "Shall I reply to her and thank her for the number then?" The things you do for a man. I muttered under my breath. I am a mug messaging her for him.

"Yeah go ahead, I'll text him." Damian shouted from bathroom.

We walked down to breakfast and met the gang, David was singing at the top of his lungs "I got that summertime summertime sadness!!!!!" It was Paddy's favorite song, and the two of them did a mini finger pointing rave in the middle of the restaurant, normally that would sound out of place but in Vegas they weirdly blended in.

"Plan tonight guys?" Emily asked. "Can we go for dinner? I want to go to Hooters and get one of those tops!"

Euan smiled at her giving her a wink, Euan loved her interest in hooters, but like any other man on the planet, he wanted to go to Hooters too.

"YES! We are so going there! I want those shorts for dancing." Sophia said.

"Hooters it is then!" David looked delighted.

We sat in the sun for a couple of hours and drank some cocktails. Damian was frantically texting on his phone again.

"Babe, did they get back to you about your card holder?" I said looking over at him.

"Yes I got it!" he snapped.

"You got it?" how the hell did he manage that, we've only been here a few hours?"

"Yes Bradley dropped it at reception he was passing by. I went to collect it when I went to the bathroom. I've put the joint card back in your handbag." he said nonchalantly.

"Aw that was nice of him." I said and went back to my book. Reading the book on holiday was not something I actually thought would happen. However I need to look as normal and as relaxed as possible. Breathe Gabriella breathe, one, two, three, four, five, I hate counting to ten it doesn't ever help, Six, seven, eight, nine, ten. Compose yourself and don't rise to bait. He is being a twat, he is acting like a twat and he is treating everyone like twats. This does not mean that you have to follow suit. You are not a twat and this out of character behaviour will not affect your holiday. You've worked hard all year for this and waited a long time for the break. Just breathe and read the book. We have so much to look forward to and you have been looking forward to having nice tanned glowing skin. This is going to work out, it will be fine.

"Gabby?" Sophia looked at me strangely. "What are you thinking about?" "Me?" I slightly jumped out of my skin "Nothing just work. I wanted to take a moment to feel the heat on my skin and appreciate the sun, why what's up?" I hope she didn't see me counting to ten. I couldn't admit fully to her what is going on; it would only make matters worse. Damian wasn't a bad person he was just having a bad moment, they didn't need to know the ins and outs.

"Nothing doll, I just seen you thinking and thought I'd say hiya." she was so sweet sometimes but I knew she knew something was going on.

"What are we going to wear tonight?" she asked.

"I'm just going to put on my cute white skirt and the little top, its hooters so not too fancy but if we decide to go out then I can make it work for both." I replied.

"Good plan, I'll do something similar. Maybe my crop top and shorts with wedges."

I hadn't eaten properly for days; the thought of eating an American super-size burger was turning my stomach. The only good thing is I can blame alcohol, I was already 5 pounds down and we weren't even five days into the holiday. It really was nothing to stress about I did want to be skinnier. Hooters Vegas was amazing, the girls were so hot. And for a woman to say that really means something, the boys were in their element. The girls and I bought t shirts and hot pants and vowed to be Hooters girls this year for Halloween. Damian and I have decided to have a house party this year – we'll just need to figure out something the boys can dress up as too.

We sat at a massive round table. I had Tilly one side and Damian the other. Without hesitation David, Paddy, Sophia, Euan and Emily ordered cocktails. I couldn't stomach it; my nerves were starting to get the better of me, that's if it was nerves. It could've been alcohol, I was a crap drinker and I was giving it a really good go this holiday but I needed a break. So, I ordered a coke, Damian and Tilly ordered water. At least I wasn't the only one in the no alcohol club.

Damian rudely texted non-stop on his phone at the table, it was beyond obvious how off he was being.

"Damian babe," I whispered. "Can you stop texting your being really rude."

Damian replied, "Tilly is on her phone are you going to give her into trouble too mum?" and he chuckled with Tilly.

"Funny guys, I'm just saying we are all sitting here together and it's like I'm stuck in the middle of some secret conversation." I nervously tried to laugh off their comments.

I ate ¼ of my burger. It was not as satisfying as it looked on the plate. It was no criticism of the food it was definitely me, I felt ill. The thought of food made my stomach turn. When we finished dinner, we planned to go back to the casino and win some money.

"Guys?" I said quietly. "I'm not feeling very well, I hope you don't mind but I'm going to go home to bed. I think the partying and drinking is getting the better of me and I need a good sleep."

"Sleep? Sistaaa ? you crazy ? We in VEGAS MAN!" David was tipsy and hugging me. "Don't be a party pooper we want you to stay out."

"David, if the lightweight is tired she'd tired. Let her get home to bed and she can save her energy for tomorrow." Sophia winked at me.

I don't know why I'm looking at Damian, there's no way he is going to come home with me.

"Babe, no way, I'm staying out for a bit. I won't be late though." he said and kissed my head.

I left the group whilst they cheered and whistled at me walking towards the elevator. Gabriella is tired, confused and lost. Tears began running down my face and I tried to casually wipe them as a couple in the lift basically had sex in front of me. As I got to the hotel room, the tears were unstoppable. Why was I crying? I was so tired and probably hungry the thought of food made me sick, I was shaky and a grey colour swept over my face. Oh god not again. Bluuggghhh, I was sick again. I was never sick, could I be pregnant? Nah definitely not I was on the pill and we were still having sex but maybe not to the extent that would make that a possibility. I think the honeymoon phase had well and truly passed after five years. I threw water on my face and took my makeup off. Gabriella what is going on? That was the question, what was actually going on? Is it me? Do you think anyone else notices the way Damian is treating me? Or his attitude towards everyone? Maybe I'm too highly strung and need to chill out? I wasn't very good at partying; I worked nearly 60 hours a week and constantly ran after Damian and Penny, I never had the energy to party at home. Maybe Damian does have the energy? I brushed my teeth and slipped on my nightie and got into bed. It was 12.37am in Vegas and I was alone in bed again. Maybe if I close my eyes tight enough, I'll sleep for more than three hours and it won't feel like Damian has stayed out all night again.

Chapter 22

Day five in Vegas and I have no idea whether I am coming or going. I'm now about seven pounds down, and I have no idea if he's ok. Damian was the love of my life, my rock, the reason I wanted to do so well in our lives, if he was down I had to help him.

I couldn't help but think he was crumbling under the social pressure to get married. I suppose I'm scared that he doesn't want to marry me, but surely that isn't what the issue is.

It was 6am and the door opened slowly, the hotel room was dark and cold. "Hey babe, are you up?" He croaked with his face close to mine. All I could smell was jack Daniels on his breath. "I'm fine, are you ok?" I looked at him hoping for an answer, surely, he must know he is destroying me with worry.

"I'm fine babe, just tired, come here." He lay down beside me and I cuddled into his chest.

Within seconds he was sleeping. I knew he needed a blow out, he was under so much pressure at work and he had been looking forward to this for so long. The holiday was far from perfect the niggles in the group were unavoidable, but something is wrong and I feel sick. I can't remember the last time I ate proper food, am I hungry? I don't even know I'm just nervous.

Three hours passed and I couldn't lie there anymore, the room was empty even though we were lying there together. What will make me happy right now? Sunshine! I showered and put on my day five bikini. I was skinnier, but not in that I've been working out I look awesome skinny, I was scrawny and I looked ill. My face looked awful, and although I am not one of those lets wear makeup to the pool girls, today had to be an exception, I cannot be questioned by the guys anymore.

He followed me down to the pool and I lay in the sun with my eyes closed. David and Sophia were downing daiquiris like water, Paddy and Euan were chilling with some beers whilst Damian again texted relentlessly on his phone. At that point Tilly had gone for a walk. I was trying to play it cool behind my sunglasses but I am not ok at all. Maybe a drink will help,

"Paddy add me in the next round, I need to get on it I must be on a five-day hangover, how are we gonna manage to ten days" I chuckled.

"Well sweetie we're just gonna have to try and make that happen, Damian you in?" He asked.

"Yeah ok." Damian answered without looking up and immediately went back to texting on his phone. Ignorant bastard! I wish he wasn't so bloody rude. Breakdown or not at least don't let it affect anyone else, jesus honestly. My patience was wearing out and I was completely embarrassed with his antics.

"Thanks Paddy, you're some guy!" I said sipping my daiquiri, god I need this. "What does everyone want to do tonight?"

"Well darling were gonna go to that steak place in PH and then out t 1OAK, how does that sound my little Kardashian?" Euan always jested I was Kim K, but I did love her so I was happy to take the compliment.

"It sounds amazing pal! I can't wait." I say smiling at him like I'm the winning an oscar for my acting skills.

Just as I put my drink down Tilly came back, "where have you been babe?"

"I just booked to get my hair blow dried at 5pm. I can't be bothered doing it myself and I think it would be a lot easier."

"Good plan, I'll get mines done on Thursday, just let me know how much it is?"

"No worries, I'll do that. Paddy can you grab me a drink?" she asked him sweetly. I couldn't get my head around those two, they had been dating for around two years, and although they are sleeping in different rooms and no longer together, they were so civil and he still treated her like a princess. Paddy was a decent guy; he earned good money and had good morals. Tilly's dad loved him and he was such a strong player in their company, what was the problem?

Like I should be focusing on that anyways, Damian was here in body; that was about it. He hardly even speaks when he is around everyone, but then when we are alone it's like nothing changed. He's always been a particular guy but I still don't think that's normal.

"Right guys, I'm going to get my hair done, what time will we meet?" Tilly stood up and started packing her things.

"8.30pm?" Emily threw back her drink, "I hope I'm not too drunk to eat!!! This restaurant is amazing! Remember girlies tonight is super glam night!"

I sat on the steps of the pool sipping my third daiquiri, "ok so shall we stay here till about 6pm? Then I'll head up and get ready?"

"Sounds like a plan sis!" Sophia and David were professionals at this; she must've been about seven drinks down and dancing in the pool, whilst David sort of did this weird dance/rave at the side. They were something else honestly; I couldn't help but smile at them, they were so happy. Deep down I was a little bit jealous.

Within ten minutes Damian stood up, "right guys I'm away upstairs for a bit I'll catch you all later." He took the key out my bag and went to walk away.

"What? Why?" I asked I felt like the ground was swallowing me up, why would he want to go upstairs?

"I'm just tired G, see you soon." And he walked away.

I felt sick, my head was spinning and I couldn't think straight. Sipping the drink down I sat back on the steps. Trying to hide that I was shaking I carried on smiling as everyone danced and splashed around. This hotel was stunning, the sun was unbelievable on my skin, and everyone looked so happy. Meanwhile I was breaking down inside.

He was with her; I knew he was I could feel it with every ounce of me. My heart was heavy and I felt sore. What am I going to do? I literally can't take this anymore I had to admit it to myself, he had to be with her, It doesn't make physical sense why they would leave at the same time. I needed to investigate this.

Standing up and drying myself off Emily cornered me, "where do you think you're going?"

"I'm just going upstairs doll, need to get started on this hair, it's gonna take ages." I avoided looking right at her, I couldn't let them know I was about to break.

"I don't think that's a good idea babe."

I stopped, "What? Why the hell not? I'm only going to wash my hair, what else could be possibly wrong?" I asked.

"Nothing, I just don't think you should go, I think it's a mistake."

"A mistake?" What the hell was she trying to say? She surely doesn't think this too?

"Yes dolly; we're all having so much fun. Why would you want to leave? There no need to, and I just don't think you should go."

Was she hell stopping me from finding out this, "well I need to go sort myself out, I'll see you soon." I was on a mission, and if it kills me I was going to find out what the hell was going on, regardless of anyone else's opinion.

I trembled walking into the salon. Please be here, please be here, please be here. Please let me be wrong about this.

"Can I help you ma'am," the receptionist asked.

"em, yeah I'm looking for my friend Tilly, is she here?" Be cool Gabriella be cool, I was so not cool.

"I'm sorry mam I don't think she's here." My heart sank, I was right, but if she's not here then where the fuck is she. Oh my god. Was I going to – Oh god.

Another stylist came to the desk, "sorry mam I was confused, she's here." She walked me into the salon and Tilly was having her hair dried.

"Hey doll, I just came to see how you were getting on, thought you were gonna text me about the hair price?" I tried to act normal, but I felt so relieved, but wow I am a bad person. How could I think that about her?

"sorry Hun," she didn't look up from her phone," I'll message you once I've paid."

I walked away feeling sick, not only due to ridiculous amounts of vodka I've consumed in the last five days, but my mum was right, she was only a young girl, how could I be so cruel and think she would do that, this is getting ridiculous. Damian really does need my help and support and I am a psychotic mess.

I got upstairs and opened the door to the hotel room; Damian was sitting upright in complete darkness.

"Why are you sitting in the dark?" how weird?

"I just wanted to; I needed to clear my head."

I sat beside him, "is everything alright? I'm really worried about you? What's wrong?"

"I'm fine, listen I was thinking about tonight, let's not go for dinner?"

"Not go for dinner? Why? Do you not want to see anyone?"

"I think we need some time just us, why don't you wash your hair as planned, I'll towel dry it to help you, then I'll get showered and we can order room service and watch a movie. We can meet them later if were still up for it."

"em, yeah ok are you sure?" He nodded at me. "I'll get in the shower then."

I turned and walked into the shower room, why are my hands so unsteady, I can't stop shaking, I wanted to be sick. He is ok Gabriella, he wants just us. We were good at this and we do love each other. He's not with her, that poor girl was getting her hair done and your man is here needing you to be there for him. Nothing is wrong.

I stood under the water tears rolling fast. Ten minutes passed and I let the water fall over me, I was so broken by him being broken, why was I not strong enough to hold us together, I washed my hair and cried some more. The mirror was steamed up and I could no longer see my panda eyes. At least I had a tan; it was harder to see the greyness. Now Gabriella be strong and give your man a hug. I slipped on my black cotton nightie, which was a lot cuter than it sounds; it was short and showed my small cleavage off. I put the comfortable hotel dressing gown on and wrapped my hair in a towel. God there was a lot of hair too; Krystal did my hair really well, I owed her big time.

"That's me out Mr." I walked into the room and he smiled at me from the bed, I hugged him close. I wish this moment felt better than it was, he towered above me snuggling my head into his chest. I do not feel close to him at all right now.

"right, here's the remote, pick a movie and I'll be out soon."

I felt tiny in the middle of the huge bed, we had made it to Vegas together, good or bad, it was me and Damian. Why did I feel so insecure, he wanted to party and have fun, what gives me the right to stop that? I mean come on I was being ridiculous, he didn't have a bad bone in his body.

And just to my left, was his phone, my heart raced, I can't. I looked away. I can't be that girl, I mean if he's left it of course he wouldn't mean to, I mean? He would check my phone? Wouldn't he? If I didn't check I would only feel worse.

I lifted his iPhone and swiped the screen open, he had no password. I mean its 2014 everyone has a password but he's not that kind of guy, he obviously has nothing to hide. I'm only checking so that I've checked there gonna be nothing there. It's really not a big deal at all.

Whatsapp – nothing, just mates, car chat, mum and dad checking on us.

Facebook messenger – nothing

Email - nothing

I was acting properly psychotic now, if he comes out that shower I am toast. I mean surely you wouldn't text? Would you?

SMS -

Hey gorgeous, I am so happy you are getting your hair done, can't wait to see you and be with you again tonight. PS please delete this message so Gabriella doesn't see it! XX

The message was to Tilly – Tilly, as in Tilly who was getting her hair done, Tilly who made a fool of me before Calvin, and Tilly who completely excluded herself from the girls and got her own room. Oh my god, I was choking on fear, they . . . they have . . . oh my god I can't breathe.

. . . . . .

I threw the towel off my head and I threw the bathroom door open, Damian opened the shower door in shock he was covered in shampoo, the water was still running. "G, what the fuck are you doing?" He looked at me angrily.

"Is this why I feel like this???? Is this why I can't eat or talk or breathe? Is this why you ignore me in front of the group and act normal when we're here? Damian? Have you . . .?"

Tears fell down my face and I was fragile, I was breaking into a million pieces right in front of his face.

"She's my mate!" He yelled.

"Mate? Are you fucking serious? You don't message Sophia or Emily like that!" I could hardly stand.

I threw the phone with every ounce of my strength on the marble tiles at the bottom of the shower floor. I hoped it fucking broke.

I had to get away from him, I need Sophia, I need my mum, I need to run away. I put my half my belongings the separated money and lifted my bag. I stormed out the room, in my nightie and still in my hotel dressing gown. My real hair was in waves and my extensions straight, when the minute your whole life falls apart something magical happens and you never look good and by god I didn't. I couldn't stand still; the tears were falling like someone was pouring water out of my eyes and I was pacing the floor outside the elevator. There were around fifteen Chinese tourists looking at me with their cameras, just another Vegas disaster, the way down was worse, because I knew they were talking about how much of a mess I was but I needed Sophia. I don't even have shoes on; it'll be ok once I get to her. There's and explanation for this, it can't be true.

When I got to the pool entrance security didn't even question me as I walked through. I was like a woman possessed trying to get to Sophia.

I got near the back-left pool and as I approached I could see people everywhere, there was a huge stag party and I could see David jumping in the pool. As is got close Sophia was at the bottom of the stairs in the water, before I even spoke she turned around and stood up and said, "Is it true?"

I fell to my knees, sobbing. It was true and it wasn't news to anyone but me.

It felt like my chest was being crushed into one of those giant car compressors. I couldn't catch my breath, I was sobbing and I couldn't see anything. I was at the pool in the middle of the Aria hotel in Las Vegas curled up in a ball. Sophia and Emily ran out of the pool to me and before I could even lift my head Euan scooped me into his arms and held me. "It's ok wee pal, it's ok. It's ok, it's ok." I felt so fragile, like someone had just broken every piece of me, I wasn't insane, it was real and everybody knew it. I was humiliated.

Sophia was screaming but I couldn't make out what she was saying, she had red mist over her eyes. "They will pay for this! They will pay for this! I promise you Gabby! Don't worry." She ran with Emily to Tilly's hotel room. What they were going to do I wasn't sure.

"Can you fucking believe this, how could she do that to her? If it wasn't for Gabriella she wouldn't even be here!' Sophia caught her breathe and they both stood in the lift silent. "I knew when she changed her room something was up! And that night after the Chippendales one minute me and David we are taking shots at the bar with the couple next to us and literally two minutes after . . . they both disappeared. Aww poor Gabby. . ." Sophia was angry but a huge sadness crossed her face and Emily had tears rolling down. "I don't know what were gonna do when we get here but I hope we can get some answers!" Emily was trying to be positive. "We'll make sure that Gabriella is ok after we sort this out."

When they reached the door of her hotel room Sophia stopped. "I'd better take the lid off this Daiquiri, so when she opens the door I can throw it in her face before I decide what to do next!'

"Good Plan!" Emily said.

"Open the door you fucking HOMEWRECKERRRRRRRRRR!!!! HOW THE FUCK COULD YOU DO THIS!! YOU STUPID TRAMP!! YOU HAVE NO CLASS!!!!!!" Sophia kicked and punched the door, she was angry and crying. "How could they do this to all of us?" Emily wiped her tears and then her own. "I don't know babe, but we need to be there for Gabriella."

Euan held me so tightly in my hotel dressing gown, everyone was staring at me. I couldn't make out their faces but I knew they could feel my pain.

"I'm gonna go and see Damian, if anything he owes me an explanation, he's meant to be my best mate. I love you sis." David said as he kissed me on the forehead and began walking back to our hotel room. "What can I do?" Paddy asked, he was so confused and shocked. "Do you want me to get you a drink or something?" I couldn't speak; I was focusing on breathing and trying to calm down. I couldn't feel anything. I snuggled so deep into Euan's neck he was wet with my tears.

"Go and get her a daiquiri, we need to take the edge off the shock. This is bad mate." He whispered. Paddy came back with a daiquiri and I began sipping the drink, my hair was wet and it started to sink in that I was the only person at the pool in their pyjamas. I had hoped this was standard Vegas practice. When your whole world ends they don't give you a heads up to dress for the occasion.

I wiped my tears and thanked Euan for helping me. "Listen pal, this is only step one. We still don't know what's going to happen next. "I began sobbing again and he stood up lifting me off the ground like a princess, and in one swift movement he threw me into the middle of the pool. Everyone around the pool laughed, everyone being a large stag party from Liverpool and a couple of American's on vacation. I dragged myself out throwing my dressing gown onto the handrail, my little nightdress stuck to my skin and I shoved Euan while he put a towel around me. "We all knew darling. We just didn't have any proof to tell you. I was so scared that by telling you we would push you closer to him and you wouldn't believe it. We didn't keep it from you, we just needed the right time, and we were going to do it tonight but I just don't know what to say, but I love you so much. You're my best friend and he is the biggest cunt walking. This isn't the end."

David stood outside the door before acknowledging Damian of his presence. "One, two, three." He said whispering to himself before ringing the bell. Damian opened the door and let him in. His suitcase was on the floor and it looked like he was packing. "Damian! What the fuck?" David looked at him saddened by his actions. "How could you do that to Gabby? How can you . . . how could you do it to us? I thought our friendship was real? I thought you were my best mate? When did you become this person? What have you done? What is going on?" Damian shrugged putting more of his clothes into the suitcase. "Game over; might as well leave."

"Leave? And go where? What about Gabriella? You can't just leave her here and do this? Look you've made a mistake but don't do this?" Damian zipped the suitcase and walked out of the door pushing David to the side, he walked down the corridor without as much as saying goodbye. "Damian, don't do this!"

-

David and the girls came back to the pool with no answers. He had left, where to no one knew. I honestly thought we would've talked again, I thought he would've consoled me and apologized, but he's gone, how can we ever be together again. I genuinely thought he respected me as person at the very least, maybe he just wants to give me space and he'll explain later.

"Paddy we need some more drinks!" Sophia shouted. I was there in body but nothing else. As shock took over a couple of the stags came and sat beside me. "Awrite errr kid?" the scouse lad asked. "I'm fine I mumbled or at least I will be."

"We seen that lad since day one and thought he was a weirdo. He never spoke to anyone and just sat on his phone. Any lad would be mad to do that to you. Although we don't actually know, we have a pretty good idea." They were sweet and obviously trying to make me feel better considering I'd just had a very public meltdown.

After a few drinks David and Euan took me to reception. "We think we need to change the keys to your room, if he's decided to leave he can leave, you can stay with me and Sophia in our room. But I don't want him coming back and staying there he doesn't deserve it." David explained the situation to the reception staff and it only took $100 for them to change the keys and make the room on my name only.

The boys organized everything; they decided that it would be better for us to all chill and have a few drinks in David and Sophia's room. We ordered room service and drank the champagne Damian and I had bought for our room. The girls collected all of my things for me, I couldn't go back there. The room was spinning with the champagne and even though something horrendous had just happened, everyone was in better spirits. The boys were dancing and jumping on the bed, and the girls were sitting cuddled around me. I felt like a child being monitored, but I didn't want them to leave my side, this was my safety blanket.

"You ok my wee pal?" Euan came over and hugged me like he wasn't going to let me go. I immediately burst back into tears. "Euan, fuck sake man you don't need to make her worse." Sophia mothered me and wiped my face. "Give her a minute, talk about something positive."

"Wait, are you still wearing that fucking shitey ring!! It's not even a diamond. For god sake Gabriella I thought you had high standards." Euan took my commitment ring from my hand and the boys deliberated on what to do with it. "Gabby, come here!" Euan, Paddy and David walked me into the marble bathroom, "we don't need this cheap reminder of a fake person!" Between him and David they broke the ring into pieces and put it down the toilet. Then each of the boys peed on it. I obviously did not stay to watch that part. "That's what he deserves, absolute scum bag!" Euan shouted as he danced back into the room pouring another vodka.

"I feel so humiliated. How can they just waltz off together like I didn't exist?" It was weird I was talking but I wasn't make any noise. "How could he- how could he lie straight to my face. I said I didn't want to go, I asked him to change our plans. Soph I asked him to take care of me, and never to lie to me. I at least would've had a chance to put myself first; I at least would have had a chance to not go through this embarrassment. Soph" I took another swig of my champagne. "If they can humiliate me, I'll humiliate them!"

I opened face book and posted. Damian Mclaughlin is shagging Tilly O'Donaghue! I can't believe it!

Normally I would never do something like this, but normally people don't do what they do either. Immediately my phone started going off, text messages and comments on the post. Some about karma and sympathy and then Tilly's elder sister Gaynor got involved.

Gaynor: Stop being so childish, you need to remove this post immediately!

Gaynor: This is ridiculous you shouldn't accuse people when you don't have proof!

Gaynor: You are so petty!!

I went to reply and Sophia stopped me. "I'll handle it!" she said and began frantically messaging.

Sophia: I will tell you one thing and I will tell you one thing now, your sister is a home wrecker and they both deserve every second of this. Don't you dare tell my sister what is real and what is not because it's all out in the open here!

Gaynor: The least she can do is remove it, no one else needs to know.

Sophia: unfortunately, Gabriella has fallen to sleep and I do not have the pass code to her phone, she has had a rough day, and if I were you I wouldn't be forcing anyone to remove or delete any posts. They are the scummiest people on the planet. Put yourself in my shoes and fuck off!

I woke up a few hours later. Am I dreaming? Is this real? I turned around and Sophia lay beside me with David on the other side. The room was dark but I didn't want to be here. I walked into the bathroom and lay on the cold marble floor; I lay there until I fell back asleep. All I just wanted to do is to wake up and be someplace else.

Chapter 23

My face was cold and the room was dark. Where was I? Why is my head so fuzzy? What happened? I stood up only to realise I was lying on the bathroom floor. Whose bathroom floor I wasn't sure. My naturally wavy/curly hair was sticking out in a fluffy mess and my straight extensions hung loose below. I was a mess, my eyes were puffy and red, and to make matters worse my face was swollen. I had cried a lot. Wait oh god, bluuuugggghhhhhh. I vomited in the toilet only for nothing to come up. I looked at the floor and my phone was under the bathmat, sixteen phone calls to mum, Billy called me? Why the hell did Billy call me was she not in Boston or something? Julia called me too? I sat for a minute to understand. I was in Sophia and David's bathroom and it had happened. It really happened, I was shaking and crying or sobbing is probably more appropriate.

Sophia pushed the bathroom door open and put her arms round me whilst I curled myself into a ball and hugged my legs.

"you ok baby?" she asked, "I don't know what to say, I am as shocked as you are. . .It's Wednesday, so we just need to make a decision what you want to do going forward. David checked and there's a flight leaving tomorrow and the next one is Sunday when we all are leaving. I don't know what you want to do but I don't want you travelling home alone." Sophia looked concerned but scared, she was almost crying too, I couldn't answer I just shook my head and cried some more.

"What do you want to do little lady? Come on, we need to at least get you out of here, you're not the tiger out of the hangover, get off the bathroom floor." David jested; he was testing the water to see when I would cry again, he left Sophia and I in the bathroom to figure out the next part of the plan.

I laughed, "Ok you do have a point," how were they so amazing, Superwoman Sophia, my crazy little sister managing to make me laugh and see some sort of positivity when my whole life had been hit by a comet.

She picked me up and pulled me into the room. "Enough is enough Gabby, we need a plan!"

"sissssttttaaaaaaaaaaaaaaaaaaaa." David yelled! "Feeling rough? No wonder after all those daiquiris and champagne we gave you last night, loved the

Facebook tantrum, Princess Gabriella made sure everyone knew what was going on!" he laughed rolling on the bed.

"What?" I asked. "What is it?"

"Oh god G, do you know what you did?" Sophia cackled into her water. "Paaaaaaahhhhhhhhh, look at this!!!!"

Damian Mclaughlin is shagging Tilly O'Donaghue! I can't believe it!

Oh god, that was my Facebook, and the comments had been flooding in, people from school, work colleagues, and people from our local area. Facebook messenger was full of messages and emails, and there it was a full-blown argument in the comments box between Tilly's older sister and Sophia, and but god did Sophia kick ass. She literally had nothing to say back to her. "So, erm how long did I sleep for? " I asked, I couldn't take my eyes off my phone.

"Well, it sort of happened after me and Emily were chanting CHEAT CHEAT CHEAT!! jumping on the bed and we just decided to go for the all-time burn, but to be fair you did type it, then about five minutes later you passed out and your phone locked. So, we limited the damage with Tilly's arsehole sister and thought it was best to let you rest." Sophia had the strangest smirk on her face, but I knew she was so proud of her kick ass efforts with Tilly's sister.

Scrolling through my messages was emotional. There were messages from Tilly's mum, 'you watch when you get to Manchester because I'll be there waiting for you, how dare you do that to my daughter!'

That hurt a lot, they were one of my favourite and best customers, why would I have ever planned to hurt her daughter, she's the one away with the love of my life, I was sinking my heart was sore and the tears started again. I don't deserve to be treated like this.

"Gabby, come on now, you look like a little bedraggled lion." David hugged me and passed me some water. "It's done now, so don't beat yourself up, if anything it's the least they deserved. what will make you happy today, we don't need to make any decisions just yet, lets enjoy the day the best we can." he squeezed my shoulders and walked to the bathroom and turned on the shower.

What would make me happy? em not losing the love of my life to my fake best friend maybe? Not lying on the bathroom crying after posting on Facebook that my picture perfect happy life is actually a load of crap, I am such an idiot. My hair is a mess, my face is a mess. Wait, my hair! I'll go get my hair done. That will make me happy, surely.

"Soph, I'm gonna go get my hair done, it'll make me feel better and I'll meet you guys at the pool, how does that sound?"

"You sound chirpy, ok doll, you do that, DAVID!! GET OUT THE SHOWER GABRIELLA IS GOING TO GET HER HAIR DONE!" she yelled through, David came out of the bathroom in a towel, " I suppose I'll get ready in here then," he looked at Sophia a little unhappy.
"She needs this more than you David!" Sophia whispered as I walked into the shower room.

I put on some fresh clothes and tied my hair up the best I could. Sophia and David have made space for me in their hotel room. I don't know any couple that would do that. `But I suppose I don't know anyone this has happened to, I love them both so much.

This was the scariest thing that ever happened to me. Only last week we viewed our dream sandstone house, the basement was our mega wardrobe and spa bathroom/sauna. Did I imagine it? Did we not plan our wedding in Dubai and talk about who was going to be there and why? And also, about how we didn't need fuss we just needed us and Penny? This wasn't a dream; this was a real-life nightmare.

"Hi Mum," I croaked.

"Are you ok darling? I see it was an eventful day yesterday? I spoke to your sister, I am so glad she is there." my mum was heartbroken, I could just tell.

"I don't know mum, what happened? I just feel sick, I can hardly breathe."

"I know darling. Me and your auntie Madeline are worried sick. But we think you should stay in Vegas, you don't know anyone, and you don't have to face anything just yet. So why don't you laugh if you want to laugh, cry if you want to cry and try to piece your thoughts together for what you think is best to do next. You're a brave girl and I love you."

"Mum I don't understand, how? Why? Why did I not see this coming? Am I that stupid?" I croaked.

"No darling, some people just do bad things, but hell mend them. Let's try to be positive; what are you going to do today? I think you should go to the pool, put your sunglasses on and read your book."

"I'm going to get my hair done, I look a mess. Not that I'll feel better but at least I won't look like a lion.'
"Good girl"

"Mum? What if I cry?" I asked. I was so emotional.

"Darling if you feel like crying you cry ok?" mum always knew best. I wish she was here.

"Ok. I love you."

"I love you more darling, and smile. The truth is out now we move forward. Call me soon." And she hung up.

Mum was in Spain, phone calls from Las Vegas to Spain, to Boston, to Glasgow. I was going to have a great phone bill this month. It felt like I was walking in slo mo towards the salon. Nothing seemed real, the slot machines were muffled and it felt like everyone around me was looking at me. It was like the Truman show. I all of a sudden became that person that wore sun glasses inside. But like mum said it's not like I know anyone, and technically my whole life just blew up, sunglasses inside is the very least of my worries.

"Hi Mam, how can we help you?" the receptionist asked. I wonder if they remembered me from yesterday.

"Em, can I have a wash and blow dry please?" I could hardly talk; I tried to clear my throat for the next question.

"Which time mam?" she asked.

"Is now possible?" my hand were shaking under the desk, please say yes, I don't know what else to do or where else to go if you say no.

"Let me check." the receptionist went behind the wall and came back around, "of course mam, how are you today?"

How am I? One . . . two . . . three. I burst into tears and my incompetency to breathe came back.

"Oh my god! i . . i . . .i . . . I'm not ok at all, I just found my boyfriend of five years has been sleeping with my best friend." I held my head in my hands, and the tears were falling on the floor in a small puddle.

"Oh my mam, ok, let's take you to Janice, she will make your hair fabulous and you will feel amazing!"

I am literally the most humiliated person in the world, how could I even just say that? I sat on the chair staring at my overly red puffy face, still wet with tears which I have wiped away the best I could.

"Good morning Mam," Janice danced over not noticing my face, "what will we do with you today?" and then she noticed. "oh my baby? You ok? What's wrong?"

And like word vomit I spilled the sad story of Damian and Tilly. "she was here last night." I wailed; I came to check because I thought they were together and she was there." I was struggling to keep my breath consistent. "I came to check, because I. . ."

"Girl, you don't mean that girl who sat over there with Jonathan last night? Nu ah! She was nasty! I could just tell there was something not right about her. She sat on her phone the whole time. What a bitch, who even does that to her friends? And him? Him? he seriously made a mistake girl! Ok this is what we are going to do, Candice is gonna take you for a shampoo, and make sure she gets the massage seats and a full treatment, don't leave anything out this girl needs to de stress."

Janice winked at me as the girls took me over to the chair; I lay for fifteen minutes whilst the chair massaged my bones. Candice was amazing she massaged my head and hands and put on low spa music, it was like she knew my aura was damaged and she was trying to put me back together.

"Gabriella?" Janice shouted, "do you like champagne girl? We are celebrating!"

I nodded and laughed, this was a real-life movie. My lion hair was washed and smoothed and when I reached the chair a tall crystal glass held the cold champagne.

"To the bitches that take the mediocre men from our lives!" Janice shouted and necked her champagne.

"Cheers." I said, I couldn't help but laugh although nothing was funny about my life right now.

Janice didn't ask what I wanted she said I needed awesome hair to take the day and laughed. She was amazing, gorgeous long dark hair and in her forties. She had a daughter and a partner. Her first husband had left her to bring up her daughter alone, she was strong and resilient. I think she was Mexican or Spanish, but she was beautiful, she made me feel so calm.

"If that monster comes back were gonna use peroxide instead of shampoo. She can sue! the girl is a bitch and she deserves it!" everyone in the salon was around me talking about the situation like they'd just read the latest OK magazine, they knew exactly which client it was and they were all on my side. This was surreal.

Sophia: Babe, were at the pool, come get us when you are done xxxxx

G: ok doll, weirdly having fun in the salon. Won't be long. X

And Janice did my hair, I felt like Beyoncé, my hair was volumized and wavey with gorgeous curls falling down my shoulders. It was thirty-six degrees outside but I looked like I was about to do a photo shoot. I bounced when I walked and as I came out of the salon I seen bracelets for sale, one of them stared right at me. Karma: What goes around comes around. Wear your bracelet as a reminder to keep in the circle positive, peaceful and loving.

I put it on and paid my bill. Grandad would make sure karma found them, no matter how hard this next part was. I hugged the girls and thanked them for the champagne and promised I would be back to get my hair done again before I left.

I couldn't believe the support from them, whether I was paying them or not that was unbelievable. I was buzzing walking towards the pool.

"Gabriella Johnston!! wheet wheeeeeeeeeewwwwwww!!!" Sophia shouted across the pool, every single person turned around and looked at me. Thank god is' ok to wear sunglasses outside. I was nervous but managed to control my walk as I got beside the group, Euan hugged me and Emily raised her glass.

"Would you like a daiquiri?" Sophia asked, pulling me down at the side of the pool. "you look stunning!" she grinned and hugged me tight.

"You're gonna be ok, we've got you." she passed me a daiquiri and I took a sip. I will be alright, I just don't know when.

Minutes after the scouse stag party joined our group. "You alright lass? Your looking cracking!" one of them said to me, I have no idea how to handle this.

Chapter 24

It felt as though everyone knew I was broken, I was fragile and vulnerable. All day Euan, Paddy and David ran around getting me drinks and kept the banter going with the scouse stag party. My head was spinning with the opinions of people around the pool, I couldn't be mad everyone knew because to be honest it was me who showed up crying in my dressing gown yesterday. "He never looked at you." one of the boys said, "You're way too pretty for him she was fake looking." another said.

"We all knew," Sophia said, "Ok well we didn't know one hundred per cent but we had a good idea. David seen Damian texting her at the airport, and the night after the Chippendales David and I were taking shots at the bar with a wedding party and when we walked back ten minutes later they were gone. I wanted to assume they'd gone to bed but my gut told me something else." She tailed off.

I was sick inside, my stomach turning. The only thing I could manage was vodka. He was still sleeping with me at the same time. I liked how no one could see my eyes on these sunglasses. Thank god for polarized gold Michael Kors. I was shaking underneath my vodka confidence, every inch of me wanted to lie in a dark room and cry, but I couldn't let everyone down, he let me down, he let them down. They very least they deserved was for me to at least try to appreciate what they are doing for me. Everyone in the group looked so much more relaxed, the tension had lifted and it was like a weight was off everyone's shoulders, how could they have known before? I knew Sophia would've kept it from me for a good reason. The vodka numbed me and I took in my surroundings, the pool was lively and people were laughing, I knew they were relaxing from their everyday jobs and letting go of all of their stress. I couldn't help but feel a pang of jealousy in knowing they could leave here and go back to their normal lives, I don't even know what my normal life is anymore, or if it even exists.

My head will not stop spinning – must be the vodka. How has this turned out to be my five star Las Vegas holiday. Everyone knows what's happened and it's all because of me; me and my stupidity, who did I actually think I was doing such a stupid thing on Facebook. What have I gained except an inbox full of sympathy messages and war between the sisters defending both sides? Although I'm not alone, I actually am alone, we came as a couple, a unit and well, where is he? Why has he not tried to see if I am ok? Why did he leave? If they were just friends why did he need to leave? It doesn't make sense. Maybe if I call my dad?

"Hi Darling, how's the holiday?"

"em, hi dad. Holiday is em well ok. . . I mean not ok. It's actually a disaster."

"I hope you girls aren't getting too drunk?" he said laughing.

"No well . . . he's gone. . . I found out that Damian was seeing my friend Tilly behind my back and I asked him about it and he just left. I haven't seen him in a couple of days and well he's just gone..."

"Right, are you ok? Are you with Sophia?"

"Yeah I'm with Sophia."

"Ok, we sometimes we need to learn hard lessons and one of those lessons is, well darling men are men. Sometimes we make stupid decisions and that's just how it is."

"What? Really?"

"Yeah darling really, it's life. Just be brave and enjoy yourself. You only have a couple of days left, give me a call when your home. Your phone bill will be through the roof."

"Ok dad, bye – love you."

"Love you, chin up."

I suppose it is that simple. Men are men and people are people. They make mistakes, they build houses with you, and buy dogs, and go holidays. But they make mistakes and it's simple and easy and you just get over it like they didn't have the right type of milk in the convenience store for you. You replace the need for that particular brand of milk with something else, easy, simple, no confusion. I feel like this is the point where I'm meant to walk away from everything and not crumble to the ground, but like my dad said men are men Gabriella you'll be just fine go along with your day.

The scouse lads were all tall and well built, they were having the time of their lives they spent most of the day chatting to us and making jokes at my expense. They did have a point though; if you were going to get dumped you might as well get dumped in Vegas. Euan was right, I'd lost weight, I had good hair and I was in Vegas with my closest pals. Bad things happen but you have to make the best of it.

One of the boys Craig chatted to me all day. I couldn't remember what it was like to flirt, or what it was like to be chatted up, it was five years since I was last single. He was tall and extremely well built with blondish hair, he was potentially taking steroids but he was cheeky, and in a time where I should be drowning in my own pool of tears but he made me laugh and complimented me. I had no idea what I was doing. The Liverpool boys begged us to go out partying with them tonight. I just knew that everyone wanted to go so I agreed.

"Gabriella, can you get in the shower please?" Sophia shouted. "You can't call mum again, she can't fix it. You might as well enjoy it while you can." "Siiiiiissssstttttttttttttaaaaaaaaaaaaaaaaa, we are counting on you! Let's get fucked up and have a good night!" David shouted. They played the music so loud the vibration from the speakers filled the bathroom, I was drunk, I couldn't think, I couldn't see and I couldn't stop the tears from falling down my cheeks. I stood in the shower for ten minutes before deciding to shave my legs. The waxing hadn't lasted as well as I'd hoped and it would make me feel better if at the very least I had clean shaven legs. I wiped the condensation from the mirrors and looked at my face. I was no longer with Damian; I don't know where he is, or what he's doing. I lost someone I don't even know and I don't know if I would find him again. How could he do that? He lied straight to my face, abused my love, my kindness and my body. Oh my god my body, I heaved in the sink. He has been sleeping with me and her on this holiday. Bleeughhhh, I vomited nothing but vodka, the thought alone was enough for me.

"GABRIIIIIIIIIIIIIEEEEEEEEEEEEEEEELLLLLLLLLLLLLLLLLLLLLLL AAAAAAAAAAAAAAAAAAAA!!!!!! PHONE!!!" David Screamed. Phone what is he talking about? "It's Craig." he chuckled I picked up the hotel room phone.
"Y'alright lass? I was thinking instead of going out with everyone else we should go out together tonight. I want to show you how a real man would treat ya?"
"Emmmm, I'm not sure." what the hell is going on, why does he want to go out with just me?
"Ok la, I'll make you a deal. We are going for a drink and we'll meet everyone after, I'll see you at 9pm downstairs."
"Ok." I was shitting myself.
"Ok, see you then." he was such a light and happy person. How was I going to get out of this?

"What did he want?" Sophia asked coming out of the bathroom in a towel. "David SHOWER!" She snapped.

"Craig wants to take me for a drink before we meet everyone tonight." I couldn't look at her because I just didn't know what was right.

"You should go! Fuck it! Damian is gone anyway; you're single, go for it! DAVID wait till you hear this!! Craig wants to take Gabriella out for a drink!!" Sophia shouted through to the bathroom.

"Are you gonna go??" he jested. "I don't see why not!"

"What are you gonna wear?" Sophia started going through my suitcase," here! This one, the green one! It'll be gorgeous with your tan."

I could go; I mean what would make my day better? Nothing could happen and we'd meet everyone after. I pulled out the new underwear I bought at Victoria's secret and started taking off the tags.

"Ooooohhhh popping tags, are we? This means business Gabby!" David was such a wind up. He didn't know what he was talking about.

"Shut up David! I just want to feel nice." I put my dress on and Sophia did my makeup, we all met down stairs and Euan pulled me aside.

"Do you know what you're doing Gabby? I mean you're a grown up but you're head really isn't in the right place. So much has happened in the last 24 hours. I don't want to worry about you more. Just stay with us."

"Euan, NO!!!! She needs to know there's life beyond this and look were in Vegas, we have five days to be carefree before we go back - . . . back to Glasgow of course." Sophia said looking at me.

"it's fine you can say it, I'm going home to a warzone. Maybe I shouldn't" "No Gabby go!! Craig! Nice to see you, here's Gabriella." She turned me towards him.

He had on a pale blue shirt and chinos, his blonde hair complimented his tan and his muscles were showing through.

"Come on la!" He took my hand and we walked out of the hotel.

"You ok?" He looked in my eyes. I nodded taking away from his gaze. "I don't know why he did that to you, but it's gonna be ok. I promise." He pulled my chin towards him and I pulled away. I couldn't be negative right now.

"Of course, it is." I giggled. "Ok no more drama talk I'm pretty done with it for one day."

Craig was a builder, he was twenty and single, and was in Las Vegas for his best mate's stag party. He'd been with his fiancé for eleven years and the boys all knew each other since school so they decided Vegas was the only place to celebrate their first friend in the group to get married. It was quite refreshing to hear all about them and their mad stories. They were really going for it in Vegas, that was for sure; although they had all taken a lot of drugs. That was not my scene at all; I was bad enough after two glasses of wine never mind taking anything stronger.

We walked into the chandelier bar in Cosmopolitan, it was beautiful everything sparkled and it made me nervous. Why is a man I don't know holding my hand and ordering me a drink the bar? I was nauseous. "Here ya go babe." he said winking at me handing me a cocktail.

"Cheers to getting rid of the people that don't deserve us." cringe, I was assuming he meant Damian. Just don't cry Gabriella no matter what happens. Craig told me dad jokes and we bought drink after drink. "Right La, shall we get out of here?" he said cheekily.

"Em sure, where is everyone?" I asked.

"I think they've went to MGM, can we nick back to my room till I grab some more cash?"

"Yeah sure, no problem.' I said. The walk back to the hotel was short, but when the air hit me outside I realized I was little giddy. This very handsome muscley man was buying me drinks and holding my hand. This was too soon, I was shaky and using my all new Vodka Vegas confidence to get me through the current hell that was my life. Ok not complete hell; he was like a real-life Chippendale. Damian is with Tilly, Damian has not tried to contact you or contact anyone else to check your wellbeing. Damian the love of your life is a liar and has left you, why are you worrying about what is right and wrong, you have four days left of Vegas and you can enjoy the time you have or you can cry for the guy that wants to sleep with you and your so called best friend at the same time. It's such a disgusting thought him doing that with her and me. "You ok la?" he said looking right in my eyes.

"Yeah of course, I'm just taking it all in, Vegas is so beautiful there's too much to look at."

"There's no point in looking at anything else la when you're here." And at that moment he grabbed my face and kissed me, ok he never kissed me he snogged my face off. I think I snogged him back. I'd lost all confidence with kissing boys and here I was on the bridge between Cosmopolitan and The Aria kissing a guy who is not Damian who I met less than twelve hours before. It wasn't illegal to enjoy the kiss, was it? I mean timing isn't great but he was a good kisser. "Come on babe, let's go back to the room and pick up some money and we can go out." He kissed my forehead and he held my hand tight as we pushed through the crowd. He was confident, and in some strange way he was taking care of me. It was like he knew how I needed to be handled; he threw a couple of dad jokes into the conversation as we got into the lift to his room. The lift was full and he squeezed my hand as we stood at the back of everyone, as soon as they left he kissed me and held me close. Was I going to do this? The thought of Damian sleeping with me and her disgusted me to extreme levels and he had left with her and made his choice. This was potentially the most extreme thing I had ever done. When we got to the hotel room, he didn't even get his money he grabbed me and picked me up; he kissed me soft and hard and called me beautiful. Gabriella the over thinker was terrified to continue. "Craig. . . Craig . . . "I can't I said pulling away from him, this is just too soon and I just don't know if this is the right thing to do. My head is everywhere." I sat on the edge of the bed and looked at him.

"Ok babe, whatever you think is right I'm ok with." he said softly.

"It's just the thought of Damian sleeping with her and me at the same time it's so gross and its only just happened, and I've never slept with someone I've just met and I-" he shhhsst my mouth and whispered in my ear. "Babe, I don't want you to do anything you don't want to do." he kissed me and I kissed him back as ran his hands up my legs, he was kneeling on the floor looking up at me sitting on the edge of the bed." it's up to you." he said cheekily winking. "I . . . I . . .really don't know. I'm so confused." he sat beside me and put his arm around me. Damian had slept with me and her at the same time, it was so disgusting. As was sleeping with someone you've just met. But in all honesty what is worse sleeping with a random that hardly knows you and owes you nothing or sharing your boyfriend with someone else's- ok decision made. "Are you ok babe?"

"Of-course I am, I've actually not been in a date like situation for years, I can't remember what it's like that's all." I didn't want to talk about it, but it's like I can't run from it. It's swallowing my every thought, and right or wrong I don't want to think about it right now. I could feel the tears filling my eyes but I refused to cry right now. I'd rushed out to date a guy I'd just met the same day, but something in me wanted to do this. I didn't want to know that Damian was the last guy to you know. So here I am in a Las Vegas hotel room with a gorgeous guy who has made a complete effort with me all day despite my psychotic circumstances and I am considering whether or not to sleep with him. I was tipsy and I had lost everything anyway it's not like this was going to impact my relationship; I didn't have one anymore anyway. "Craig?" I looked over at him he was opening a beer and passed me one.

I took a huge gulp of beer for my first time and kissed him. "I don't want to talk about it, ok?"

"Ok babe." he kissed me and grabbed me and before I knew it my green bandage dress was on the floor, so much was happening at the one time I found it hard focus. I was mesmerized by his perfectly muscley body and aftershave absorbing me. And right before I had a chance to think, he was inside me. It was a crazy moment of passion and fear. I had actually done it; I had got rid of Damian, well in that sense at least. Craig grabbed me and pushed and pulled me like nothing I had felt before. I could see his reflection in the glass wall looking out onto Las Vegas. His body was like something out of a movie, so perfect and strong, he kissed me and teased me and when it was over we did it again.

I lay in the dark room looking out at the lights of Las Vegas. Craig lay beside me sleeping. I had just had a one night stand with a man I know as Craig who is a builder from Liverpool. I found my underwear on the floor and slipped it on and went into the bathroom. It's not like I could sleep anyway, I was such a slag, and in hindsight think I used him as much as he used me. He served a purpose, knowing Damian was the last guy to sleep with me when he was doing that disgusted me. I mean at least Craig didn't buy me a commitment ring or share a mortgage. He served a purpose, It was 6am and the sun was coming up. I took one of the hotel dressing gowns and I lifted my dress from the floor.

"Thank you" I whispered kissing him on the head.

"La, you're gonna be alright I promise.' he said and lay back down.

"I know, thank you." I said and walked out of the hotel room.

The worst part was telling everyone else. Although I'm pretty sure they would have already known exactly what happened.

I slipped into David and Sophia's room and went straight in the shower. It was the first time I'd done something completely ridiculous and was not politically correct. Weirdly I felt proud, I'd finally done something for myself. Like sleeping with a complete hunky stranger was something to be proud of. But my reasoning behind it surely stood for some moral standing.

"Sisssssssstttttttttttttaaaaaaaaaaaaaaaaaaaaaa!!!" David shouted from the bedroom. "Is that you???????????????????" his face was planted in the pillow face down. They had even left my pillow wall up; they obviously thought I was coming home last night. "Well? Did you swing from the chandeliers last night??? "David sang, "Immmmmmmmmmm gonna swiiiiiinnnggg from the chandielieeerrrrrrss from the chandeiliersssssssssssssssss, iiiiiiiiiiiiiiiiiiiimmmmmmmmmmmm gonnnnaa liiiiiivvveee liike tommorrow doesnnntt exissssssssttt like it doessssnnnttt exxiiiiiiiiiiiiiiiiiiiiissssttt!" "Fuck off David; it's none of your business. But yes. I feel a little bit better." I answered back and stuck my tongue out at him.

"Shall I have breakfast with my two favourite sisters?"

"Yes please get the menu. I want to eat today." I answered.

"Got your appetite back I see. PAHHHHAHAHA "David was a prick. But I did love him loads. I know he was only messing. But in all honesty, I had just slept with a complete stranger twenty-four hours after the love of my life left me in Vegas. I wonder what today would bring.

Chapter 25

I couldn't help but feel guilty, Tilly left Paddy four weeks before, got another hotel room, and basically made an absolute fool out of him and no one is asking if he is ok. Euan took me down stairs for breakfast, he put his arm around my fragile shoulders and didn't say a word. I knew he had my back, he was like a body guard protecting me from harm.

"I think you guys should have a boy's day." I said.

"a boy's day? What? Why?" he said stuffing his face with toast.

"I feel awful that everyone is focusing on me and it happened to Paddy too. He needs to enjoy Vegas and just have a bit of a blow-out. Go shooting or go to the strip club? Do something Vegas like."

"Gabby! That sounds absolutely amazing but David and I are never getting away with that!" Euan couldn't wipe the smile from his face.

It took a bit of time to persuade the girls, but some shopping, chill out time and we would meet the boys in the club later tonight. I needed time to clear my head away from the boys. I needed a hug or maybe just to feel like everyone isn't staring at me because there is a strong chance I'd fall into a million pieces.

"ooooooooooooooooo Sheeeeeeeeeeeeeettttttttt!!! We gawn go, shooting! Gawn dranking and gawn to da striiiiiipppp club!"

"David? Why are you speaking like an American? You idiot! You're having a day out, we get it." Sophia rolled her eyes. "This is going to end in tears, and they won't be mine HA!"

"You jus jealous baby!!! We gawn have a goooooooood daaaaaaayyyyyyyyy!" David chuckled. "See ya soooon ladies." After handing us a daiquiri each the boys headed out on the boys days of boys days.

We decided to relax at the pool for a while, tiredness was catching up on me, and probably I'm hungry although I could still hardly eat. Sophia brought a me pizza, I didn't even think I could stomach a pizza, and I love pizza. I also love Damian, but this pizza would work out way better for me than Damian and I ever did. What a devastating thought me lying at the pool in the Aria in Las Vegas when no one knows where he or she is, no phone call, no check-up text, no apology and no goodbye. I didn't want to cry anymore although I had so many tears ready to drop at any second. I took a deep breath and ate a slice of pizza. It was simple and perfect, thin crust, cheese, basic, just like me, no fancy toppings or extra enhancements. Although I am as basic as a cheese pizza I'd finally managed to eat a whole slice after eight days, result.

"Well done Gabby! Is that nice?" Sophia asked like a proud mother.

"Yeah, it's fine, so I know today is a boy's day but what are we doing? This is our day too." I said looking at the girls, one either side of me still protecting my every move.

"Well dolly, what would you prefer to do, you need a break so let's make it your day." Emily asked stuffing her face with a quesadilla.

"No No No!!! I know 've been a handful this holiday and there's a lot of drama but I just want you guys to have fun. So, I'm happy to follow with what you guys want. I know I can be selfish but just not today ladies."

"ooooooohhh, that sounds like fun. I think we should stay at the pool for a bit, then go shopping and spend some money, Euan left his card ha ha. Then we could go upstairs and get some food and get ready for tonight, we can meet the guys in the club later?" Emily was giggling with excitement, everyone needed this day. Not just me.

We finished our food and slid into the pool with new daiquiris, it was the drink of choice this holiday. I couldn't help but look around and see everyone enjoying Vegas. Girls on hen parties in coordinating bikinis celebrating the next chapter in their lives. Boys going crazy taking shots and jumping in and out of the pool on heavy stag parties, rowdy but full of life and having fun. Couples enjoying people watching but living new experiences together. Everyone was sucked into the carefree party atmosphere. The mood was electric and everyone around was buzzing off the vibe, then there was us. Sophia and Emily dancing in the pool loving their days freedom from their men, laughing and being strong for me. They were just as disgusted and as disappointed in Damian as me, but they never showed their fear. They were smiling and laughing like everything was ok, like nothing else would happen when this bubble burst in three days. I idolized these girls, they were the reason for my strength and the reason I wanted everyone to have this day. I didn't want to think about the changes in my life over the last week and I didn't want to think about tomorrow. I stood out like a sore thumb at this pool. But if I keep my sunglasses on, and give a smile, I could do it for them, I wanted to, this was a way of me repaying them for their strength and loyalty as friends, as sisters, and as a family. I jumped out the pool and ordered three more daiquiris, when I returned there were four extremely tall, handsome Canadians talking to the girls.

"So, who's single out of you babes?" one of the boys asked.

"Oh, my sister Gabriella is – here she is." She said as I handed the drinks and got back into the pool.

"What's this?" I questioned laughing.

"Your single baby?" he asked again.

"yup." I said taking a large swig of my daiquiri, the first blow, smile Gabby smile.

"great, when do you girls wanna come party with us?" I couldn't remember how to do the small talk thing, luckily Sophia was full of confidence.

"party? Where do you guys wanna go? We're having a girl's day today whilst our men go enjoy Vegas on their own. We've got some tanning some shopping and some drinking to do." Sophia said confidently.

"That sounds awesome, were actually going to our friend's wedding. We actually need some plus ones if you'd want to go?"

A wedding us? As plus ones?

"Gabby?" Sophia looked at me hoping for an answer.

"I don't know guys we couldn't just turn up it wouldn't be fair we don't have a present for them."

"You don't need a present we'll drink later? Just come girls it'll be so fun." He was around 6ft 5 and was the build of an ice hockey player. He has mousey brown hair and a thick accent, was this what you were meant to do in Vegas? Go to parties with strangers? Turn up at weddings of people you don't know. I don't think I just could turn up to a wedding. Imagine hearing an I do, I felt sick at the thought of it.

"We need to go get that bracelet Soph, remember we said we'd go today." I looked at her hoping she felt my fear.

"aw of course so we did Gabs. Sorry guys wish we had more time otherwise that would've been amazing. What a cool way to get married though, how many of you are here?" She asked.

"Around thirty, were all staying in different hotels though, different people different budgets. Were only here for the weekend though. How many days are you girls here for?"

"ten." I answered straightly.

"ten!!!!! Someone is gonna die! I don't know anyone that can survive ten days in Vegas." Me neither, I suppose it comes with the package, you need to lose something in Vegas.

"Well ladies we need to change for the wedding hope you have an awesome free day. "

"They were hot Gabby, you need to get out there!" Emily whispered.

"too early Em, I've already done what I needed to do." I giggled, jeez and Gabriella Johnston did.

After a couple of hours, we got changed and headed to the shops. Emily was on a Victoria's secret spree, Sophia wanted some clothes for dancing, and I needed a new bracelet. I needed to replace the Swarovski one Damian got me that I wore every day, I just didn't want the reminder anymore. We reached the shopping mall near to the Planet Hollywood hotel. It was buzzing with people carrying large drinks at 12pm in the day. Vegas was an incredible place, everyone was carefree and let go of themselves. I couldn't wait to get into the shops, I was taking the Vegas approach, I'd be carefree towards my bonus that landed right on time.

Victoria's secret is the most beautiful shop I had ever been in. The walls were lined with the world's most beautiful women, it was every man and to be honest every woman's dream. The lingerie lined the walls in stunning silks and laces. I don't know what I needed some for but I wanted to buy them. Emily salivated over a pink one piece thinking of Euan's face when he would arrive home. It was perfect for her so girly and delicate. Euan would die she looked incredible, Sophia was in the VS sports section picking up a selection of crop tops and leggings for her dancing. All colorful and tiny sizes. Sophia had got her diet down to a tee, and boy was it worth the effort. She was petite and so toned with all of her dancing. I opted for some black lace bralet and thong set, along with a new phone case, passport cover, make up bag, body sprays, shampoo, conditioner and a perfume for work. And then onto the main event Tiffany's, we needed to go to the smaller mall next to our hotel. It was literally joined at the side, I didn't want the memory anymore and needed something to wear every day for me.

"Gabby! Wait put your bags down. We need a picture of this. We been shaaaaawwwwwwwwpin." And Shopping we had. There were Victoria's secret bags everywhere, it was like girls gone wild. "let's send it to the boys. I wonder what they are up to?" Emily said as she forwarded the message to Euan. "Girls, oh my god! Look at David he's shooting that gun. Oh my god they are crazy! Wait that was earlier? They're in a limo now and Paddy is pole dancing throwing dollars everywhere." Emily couldn't stop laughing.

"wait who are they in the limo with?" I asked giggling, those boys honestly.

"Themselves!!" She said cackling away. They're doing a tour of Vegas and then going to Sapphire the strip club! They look like they are smashed. But they've been drinking since 10am and its almost 7pm. Jeez, we should go and get ready what's the name of that club again?" Emily was high on life.

"It's Marquee. The boys are coming to get us later. I think I need a nap though. Shall we go upstairs and get ready?" I said as we reached the elevators; every time I walked into the lobby I looked around for them, were they here? Had they left? Can they see what I'm doing? I suppose I wouldn't know the answer, but I still filled with fear in case they could see me.

I slept as the girls ordered food, showering and prepping themselves for the big night ahead. David put us in touch with a promo guy who would put us on a table. The joys of being a girl in Vegas, everything was free, all we had to do was dress up and show up. Today was such an amazing day the girls were so supportive but fun at the same time, they ended every bad conversation with something good. The boys seemed to be having a whale of a time too, shooting guns, throwing dollar bills at each other in a limo and spending the best part of their evening in a strip club. Mission accomplished.

After my nap, we all were ready and headed to the club to meet the boys. The place was huge, filled with people huge tables with gigantic bottles of Vodka and champagne. Lights flashing in colors all above our heads.

"this is incredible girls!" I couldn't believe we were here. I knew people did stuff like this but I was an amateur.

"I know!!" Sophia said dancing around whilst the waiter poured us some vodkas.

"where are the boys?"

"Awww man, there's David" she said putting her hands to her head. "He is absolutely smashed.

"Siiiiiiisssssssssttttttaaaaaaaaaaaa!!!! How've you been? Did you girls look after her?" he said kissing Sophia and patting my back.

"of course, we did, we had an awesome day, but enough about us. What about you guys. How was Sapphire?" Emily giggled sipping her drink. I just knew she wanted to know how Euan was in the strip club. I trusted the boys and Euan would never hurt her, plus they were doing it for Paddy it wasn't about them.

"Well we all got dances cause we in Vegas!!!" David shouted. Emily's face dropped, and Sophia looked shocked but managed to re gain her cool instantly.

"Was it even good? Paddy you're not saying much." Sophia said bitchily.

Paddy spat his drink out with the biggest smile on his face none of us had seen from him in a long time. "Are you kidding. It was fucking amazing! Those girls were absolutely fucking beautiful!'

"not as beautiful as you Emily." Euan said trying to regain some brownie points.

"I would've spent all night in there if the boys would've let me." Paddy said sniggering.

"tell them what you did" David said hysterical. They weren't making a lot of sense they were pretty drunk and it was probably time for them to go home.

"I TRANSFERRRED TEN THOUSAND DOLLARS!! INTO MY BANK ACCOUNT SO I COULD GET ME SOME PUSSY!!!!!" Paddy screamed in the worst American accent imaginable.

"What!!"

"Paddy what the actual fuck? Is that a joke? David!!! Why did you let him do it?"

"WELL, YOU SEE MAM WE RAN INTO SOME PROBLEMS WITH THE BANK OF SCOTLAND AND THE TRANSFER WILL ONLY GO THROUGH TOMORROW." He was hysterical, laughing and joking with the boys like they were five-year-olds and done something bad.

"Paddy, come on man, I thought you were putting it into your new business? Why would you do something so insane?" I questioned him.

"BECAUSE MY FRIEND! THIS IS HOW WE VEGAS!!"

"sorry what?"

"THIS IS HOW WE VEGAS! THIS IS HOW WE VEGAS!" The boys began chanting, and all I could see was the relief on Sophia and Emily's face. Paddy had lost his soul to Vegas, it was so ridiculous but so funny at the same time, god Bless the Royal Bank of Scotland, they know how and when to stop people.

"All joking aside G, the day was amazing, we honestly had such a laugh, it's like the pressure has gone from the group and we can all just enjoy it. The boys are class too. We'll always be friends G." Euan said raising his glass to cheers, he was right, how could I manage this with anyone else?

"Gabby! When we were in Sapphire we were getting a dance, and I was just telling the girls what Vegas had been like and how it was all going. So, I obviously told them what happened to you. . ."

"David, why the fuck are you telling people, she's already told face book!" Sophia was laughing her head off. "Everyone already knows!"

"We'll Gabby, to be fair it is pretty shocking, none of us have a heard a thing from either of them. I mean where even are they?"

He did have a point. Where actually did they go? And why did they not think twice about what they left behind. The sound in the club was deafening and that all too familiar feeling of my heart dropping was coming back. This wasn't a random holiday this was my actual life and before I know it I'm gonna have to go home and face it.

"Gabby! Fucking listen to me man! I'm telling you something. These girls actually listened when I spoke to them, and . . . well I've got something to ask you?"

"Ask me what?"

"Do you want to go party with the strippers??"

"is that a joke?"

"No of course not, they genuinely feel bad for you and want to take you out to make you feel better."

Something inside said this is a good idea, go out have fun and forget it. Should I? I don't think I could handle the humiliation of someone else looking at me like they can't understand how I'm still standing. I can't I've already acted out of character this holiday, there's only so much my reputation can take before it goes too far and I can't come back from it.

"Don't think so Dave, I mean let's be serious you boys will be in your bed within the hour. And I think Emily might have a heart attack if we take Euan anywhere near those girls!"

"Good point sis. I do really love you, you know. I'm so lucky Sophia brought me into your family. You really are a sister to me."

"Love you too Dave, but your drunk. Shall we all just go home, its 1am. We're ripping it now."

We walked back to the hotel, the energy was light and carefree. I couldn't be more grateful for the people I had around me. How could I have stayed here without them? Why didn't I leave Vegas? I could only take in my surroundings and embrace what I actually have. I have no idea what my Glasgow life holds for me anymore, but have two more days to get my thoughts together and breathe, maybe even laugh. I suppose can't make myself any more embarrassed than I already have been at least that's a bonus.

Chapter 26

G!!! Today we are gonna learn how to shuffle!!" Sophia screamed dancing around the hotel room. For the first time, I had managed to sleep on the right side of the bed for more than four hours. "Calvin might have had drama but ain't no drama happening today! Woooooo!"

"You right gur! We gawn PAAATTTTAAAAYYYYY"

"Guys, this is too much to take at this time in the morning can you just chill out, I've just opened my eyes." Honestly David and Sophia have way too much energy, they're like four year olds.

"Vodka anyone?" David said standing pouring himself an extra-large vodka. Vodka is all I can taste, all I can handle. I stood brushing my teeth and Sophia danced around me. "Do I look fat today?"

"Fat?" Sophia shrieked, "Is that a joke you are ridiculously skinny, it's almost gross."

"Yeah thanks soph." I feel fat, my stomach looks bloated. "Soph out the way, Blueeeghhh." Oh my god sick again, I hope this is just vodka and not morning sickness.

"G did you just vom a bottle of vodka? Ha ha that is unbelievable, totally stinks!" Sophia said shuffling out of the bathroom, this is a whole new low.

"Soph fuck off, I feel like shit, I look like shit, oh wait. I don't look so bloated anymore, must've been the vodka. Maybe I should really brush my teeth again. Ha ha."

"You are a nutter Gabby. Let's get our freak on to Red foo!"

David strutted past the bathroom in the tiniest shorts known to man. "When I walk on by gurls be looking like . . . Go Gabby sing it to me?"

"Dam he fly!"

"Atta girl! I pimp to the beat walking down the street in my new- Hey Euan yeah yeah were coming. Waiting on Gabby, she's throwing up again."

"DAVID!!!" honestly that guy!

"What! You did! Yeah yeah we're coming, see you soon."

After struggling through my heap of clothes on top of my suitcase I found my luminous pink Victoria's secret bikini. Sophia rocked out in a similar style in yellow. Today had to be a good day, I have good people around me, I'm skinny and I can smile because no one has died and there is no drama in my life. Breathe breathe breathe.

I had never visited the Wynn before. It was beautiful stunning hallways and extravagant architecture. We walked around to Encore and the que was massive. Everyone waiting in the baking sun for a pool party with the one and only Red Foo from LMFAO. It was like living in a movie, everyone was excitable and ready to have a great day out.

"You ready for this G?" Euan asked.

"Yeah I'm ready, feels like a good day is overdue."

"No tears today ok?"

"Yup no tears."

"Bikini looks cracking by the way."

"Thanks pal."

Our table was on the right side of the pool, we had a great view of the stage and large inflatable animals were passed around us. Emily and Sophia made full use of the isntagramable snap opportunity. Four hours in everyone was drunk. We were drowning in frozen strawberry daiquiris and for a while I almost forgot where we were. There was a sea of people around, drinking dancing and laughing, and well then there was me. Hiding behind my sunglasses sipping a drink and holding my nerves. To be honest I didn't really want to be here. I want to be home with mum and Penny. I want to see Damian, I want to know what has happened to me?

For a second everything was spinning. There were no faces just a blend of people singing and dancing. I had to get out of here, so the bathroom for space. You can do this Gabriella, you can do this. Why are you stressing over bad people, why are you worrying about someone that clearly doesn't care? Why can't you just let go and enjoy yourself? You're making things worse for yourself by not taking control and enjoying the time you have. Grandad would've wanted me to enjoy every moment and opportunity, so I need to make the most of it.

As I went back to the table Sophia grabbed me. "Gabs, come join this table !! oh my god these guys are hilarious." David was twirling down of the poles beside the fountain whilst Paddy filmed him.

"This place is CRAAAAAYYYYYYY, I'm having so much FUUUUUUNNNNNNN"

If anything could make you laugh is was definitely going to be David and Sophia, so carefree and so excitable. They were amazing, I'll make an effort for them, I just need one more daiquiri. And within ten minutes I Gabriella Johnson was shuffling with a group of random strangers and actually smiling.

"G! I can't believe you just did that? I mean I know I am the better dancer but you actually did good!"

"Why thank you. Sometimes I do try."

We danced and drank and danced and ate pizza. It had to be one of the best days we've has together as sisters. We could have fun together and we didn't clash. We partied and enjoyed ourselves and out of this horrible situation had just become and incredible memory with my crazy little sister.

Chapter 27

Everyone was deflated by the drama and the extreme lifestyle of Vegas. It was our second last night. No matter how hard I tried, I could only sleep for four hours at a time.

"Gabs, let's just stay in tonight we'll get an early night and watch a movie?" Sophia casually said.

"I can't. I can't sleep and I keep getting all these Facebook messages. My brain literally won't stop."

"I know, but its ok to be confused. As for the Facebook thing, you don't need to look at your phone. And not to be the big bad wolf, but you did post it on Facebook, so what do you expect people to do? People do like you and care about you Gabby. What happened isn't exactly a normal situation is it?" Sophia said softly.

"No, but . . . I just can't stop thinking about him, is he ok? Is he still here? Why didn't he check up on me? Does he not care at all?"

"I don't know if they've left, but they're not on our booking anymore." David piped up from the lounger across from us.

"What? Really? Fucking joke!" Sophia screeched. "listen Gabs, their probably humiliated by their behavior and have went home to save face."

"Home to save face? Are you serious? What about my face? What about me?" I was crying under my sun glasses again, but what the hell? It wasn't for the first time on this trip. I was actually becoming a pro at making it look like I was wiping my face instead of my tears.

"Doll, I don't know just the same as you don't but we need to focus on what makes you feel better. I mean where would you be without us?" She winked at me.

"I know, I feel like an invalid. Everyone is messaging me saying, I can't believe it. Are you ok? You deserve better, you're such a lovely person, I really didn't expect that, I thought you were perfect for each other. He is an idiot, you'll get through this. And I'm just like how? How can I get through this? I don't even know what happened, as soon as I found the message he left? How could he leave? He didn't say anything to me Soph, he didn't say anything..."

"Aww Gabby, I know, I know how bad it is, but maybe if we just try and get a proper sleep and a nice chill night you'll feel better about everything. "She came and sat beside me and stroked my face. "If anyone can handle this it's you, and I know you'll be ok."

"I don't know if I can be ok anymore. I am trying for everyone in the group, but I am terrified to go home. I don't want to face it, I don't want to face work or tell everyone oh hi, yeah, I don't know where he is but I'm ok. I'm not ok Soph, I am going out of my mind trying to figure out what happened. How could we be together, in our house with our dog, living our life, planning our wedding and then poof, like magic he disappeared. Am I'm meant to know what's going on automatically? Or is someone going to enlighten me?"

"I'm sure you guys will talk when your home. But for now, let's lie here at the pool. Try to relax and tomorrow is our last day.' Sophia lay down and closed her eyes.

Another day, another day, another fucking day of being left here. Not knowing anything. Great!

Paddy came over and hugged me from behind. "you ok princess?" he said kissing my cheek.

"I think so. . ." I was not ok, but is it really appropriate to hold onto Paddy right now, probably not.

"I know the guys don't want to go out tonight, but I'd quite like to go a walk and maybe have some dinner? Can you come with me? We'll be the lonely-hearts club together?" he said smirking.

"Yeah, I'd like that." thank god someone wants to go out.

"No, she's staying in Paddy, she's not exactly in the best place to go out every night." Sophia shouted still lying with her eyes closed.

"Shut up Sophia I'm not staying in with you too. Go and have a night to yourself. I'll come home later."

"This girl knows how to Vegas!!!" Paddy said hi fiving me!! "We're not going crazy only dinner Soph, I'll have her back at a reasonable time."

"It's not a date Paddy!!" I shouted back at him.

'Yes, I know, but we can have dinner as friend's crazy woman." he replied.

"Ok." Paddy was such a good guy, out of everyone in the group he knew me and Damian the most, and he fitted in so well with everyone. I can't imagine what it is like to be him, the other woman's ex who works for the exs dad. Talk about awkward position. It was such a strange situation as he didn't seem phased by it at all.

I got changed and ready and chucked on a plain dress and wedges. Paddy had called to say Euan was coming, he had a tiff with Emily and wanted some peace and quiet. We walked over to a steak restaurant not too far from the hotel - it was a proper American diner, the Harley-Davidson Cafe. Considering I hadn't eaten much more than half of a chicken quesadilla in the last eight days, coming here was pretty much a wrong move. The steaks were as big as my body. Euan was half chewing a steak and giving us the pep talk on life.

"Look guys, its shit what's happened, and they two are clearly bangers. But you need to make the most of a bad situation, and Gabby, you staying here has showed me how strong a person you are. I don't know anyone that would've done it. You need to be proud of yourself for pulling through and trying to accept what's happened." He was scoffing his face whilst I sipped my cola.

"I know but Paddy has too, it's not just me. I feel like everyone keeps focusing on me when Paddy has been through it too."

"Well we all go through things in life G, but some of us handle it differently. Like me and Emily, I love that girl more than anything or anyone. I can't wait to propose to her, but sometimes she's a bit of a diva and just stamps her feet, and I think what's the fucking point in caring about this girl so much when she doesn't care for me."

"We all know that's a lie Euan, she'll be gutted you're out having dinner with us and she's in the room alone." Paddy chirped.

"She's having food with Sophia and David in the room then going to bed. Everyone is shattered." he began to yawn." I'm gonna go back and sort it out. There's no need for us to be fighting now."

"Of course, not pal, she's the one for you. I just know it." Euan threw some money on the table and kissed my head. "That's why you're my best mate, you get it. Love you." he said and walked out of the restaurant.

"Love you too." I said after him. "He's some guy! I honestly do mean it when I say I love him, he is such a good guy, even though I hated him at first." I chuckled. "Are you ok Paddy? I feel like everyone is focusing on me and no one is checking on you? Are you ok? How do you feel?"

"Of course, I am darling. You don't need to ask me. It's just been a bit weird, although I feel like I need to tell you something."

"What? Tell me what?" fuck sake honestly what else could possibly be wrong now.

"Listen, Gabby, I genuinely don't know how to say this." he looked at me in my eyes and grabbed my hands.

"Paddy, wow, listen this is not what I think should happen."

"Gabs! No!! You idiot! Listen to what I'm saying to you, now this is not going to be nice."

"What isn't?" What is he talking about?

"Gabby, I knew . . . I knew it was going on, but I wasn't in a position to tell you or any of the guys to be honest. I didn't want to hurt you and push you closer to him. I was really in a hard position watching it happen to you and I'm sorry. I really am sorry." he held my hands and looked at my face. I looked at the napkin on my lap and closed my eyes.

"How did you know?" I said under my breath.

"I saw a couple of things. . . then one night it clicked. But I wasn't in a position to tell you I really wasn't."

"Can you just tell me what you seen." I couldn't take another breath, I wasn't dreaming. This happened to me, this is the reality of my dream Vegas holiday.

"When Tilly and I had words before we came, we decided to separate, and when she booked the other room she was really really happy in the office. I just went along with it because we were going to Vegas. I saw her texting him a couple of weeks before but I thought it was a friendship thing . . . Gabs? Are you listening?" he shook me, but I couldn't look up. "Then I saw them both sitting on their phones during the day and not talking to anyone in the group, so I paid attention and I watched. As one finished texting the other picked up their phone. But the nail in the coffin Gabs was the night after the Chippendales." he stopped to look at me.

"Go on." my eyes were filling up.

"Well do you remember I text you early morning asking for your room number, as Damian turned up at the door steaming drunk. He was out of it and he stank of her perfume. It was really bad, he asked if he could stay with me and he also asked if I could say we had both been at the casino and got to drunk and stayed there. Now Gabs, I didn't let him in the room, I told him I knew exactly what he was doing and I would not be a part of their lies. I said I would text you to find your room number and he could go home properly. I told him he was disgusting and nothing but a scum bag for doing that to you. . .Gabs? Gabs?" he held my hands tighter.

"What perfume was it?" I asked.

"What!" he replied.

"What perfume was it? That's all I want to know." I said sternly.

"Do you really want to know? . . . em ok It was Si, Giorgio Armani. Why is that important.?" he questioned me.

"Why is it fucking important! I don't like that fucking perfume and I knew he smelled different when he came back that morning. I didn't dream it, I actually didn't dream any of it. When I turned around as we walked to Calvin Harris and I saw them close. I knew something happened I felt it. I felt all of it, I think I watched him slip away from me. I think. . ." . . . did I let it happen? How could I be so stupid, every single sign was right in front of my face, every little feeling I had was right and here I am. Alone in Vegas – ok not alone, but I'm not with Damian. I feel like I'm suffocating myself emotionally. I don't want to believe it, they knew before they came here and they knew when and how they were doing this. The only question I had for Damian was why? Why didn't he respect me enough to at least let me go before he treated me like this?

"Gabby, don't think anymore. You don't have to; you're going to be ok. Waiter? Can we have the bill please? Listen, look at me, please look at me Gabby, you don't have to cry over this. He's gone, that horrible toxic person is gone, and she! Well the wannabe Gabriella Johnson can fuck off too. You're too good for this. Way too good for it. Thanks mate, I'll get this princess. You're ok, I promise you're ok. Let's take a walk." Paddy was in complete control of our night and for the first time. I actually felt safe.

We walked down the Vegas strip towards the Venetian. I couldn't take any of it in, he was with her and Paddy knew he has evidence. And although he hid it from me, I could understand his position. But Damian tried to get him to cover for him. Damian? My Damian? Would he do that? Would Paddy lie? As we walked down the busy strip, Paddy grabbed my hand. Something about us both being betrayed by them made it ok for us to stick together, I was shaky and my palms were sweating but I needed the comfort. I had to try and forget why this happened?

"Gabs! Look over there, it's the joker! You need a picture! Batman is your favorite." Paddy grabbed my hand, gave the guy five dollars and took a picture. "Gabs look at that. That's a cracking pic!" Paddy was smiley and full of energy but I had nothing. I was numb and running on an empty tank. He knew and I am standing here in the middle of the last Vegas strip wondering whether it is acceptable to cry again. I couldn't speak but I listened to Paddy talking about work and his plans to run his own business, he was so positive and full of life. He didn't care what Tilly did to him, he was already in the acceptance phase.

"Gabby" he clicked his fingers in my face. "Come back into the world. Hello?"

"Why does everyone lie to me?" I said bluntly.

"Not everyone lies babe." He said.

"Well you did?" I replied. I couldn't stand there and pretend I was ok, I'm not ok. I want to scream. I AM NOT FUCKING OK!!! WHY DIDN'T YOU TELL ME!!! WHY DID NO ONE CARE ABOUT ME!!! OR WHAT HAPPENED TO ME!!!!!!!!! But I stood staring quietly at the fountains at the Bellagio, I wanted to but I couldn't scream at Paddy.

"Gabby, please don't think that. I would never lie to you. It wasn't my situation to tell. Think of it from my side I was with her for two years, I work for her dad. I was told we weren't together anymore four weeks ago, and even though I said let's not go to Vegas she insisted, she pressured me, and to keep the dynamic of the group, boy girl boy girl, you know what I mean. Gabby, I promise you if I thought telling you before would've helped you I would. The thing is Tilly was your friend and Damian and I became friends as a result of that. I honestly had no choice in the matter but to go along with her plans. Like I said we were still sleeping together at the hotel in Manchester before the flight. So that says a lot more about her than you. She dumped me, forced me to go on holiday so she could take your boyfriend. Now when I say it out loud it sounds awful but at the time it didn't as bad as it was, but I was in a really hard place. I couldn't figure out who my loyalty should be with. And since I became friends with you guys, I realized I should've done something about it sooner. I haven't ever had friends like you guys, and if no one ever tells you, you are an amazing girl Gabby! Absolutely amazing and going from experience, I don't think he realizes the choice he's made. Just make sure it's too late when he does kid, ok? "

"Ok." I smiled.

"Ok? That's it?" He looked puzzled.

"yes, ok. What can I say at least you gave me an answer, at least you had the balls to state your position in the situation. Paddy I don't want them to ruin Vegas too. As if my life can't get any worse, I can't let them ruin this place for me, It's my second favorite place in the world."

"Of course not, so let's go to the high roller? We can see it all! Gabby you're allowed to smile you know. You do have things to be grateful for!"

He walked down the street with his arm around me, protecting me from the world. We ordered two large margaritas and took the escalators to the largest Wheel in the world. It was 3am and we were the only people in our carriage. We stood in silence listening to the promotional video telling us all of the facts of the high roller and watched the view expanding before us. I was mesmerized by the lights, it was an incredible sight. I stood close to the edge and peered out the way. There has to be more out there for me than Damian, please god. Give me something to hold onto.

"Gabby! Watch!! It's too high you look like your gonna fall!" he grabbed me and pulled me close to him. For a moment it felt like something should happen, should we kiss?

"Scarier things have happened Paddy." I smirked and pulled myself back from him. If Damian liked Tilly and Tilly liked Paddy and Paddy liked me, does that mean we could be compatible too? We couldn't, could we? No, I couldn't take her second-hand goods, despite how amazing Paddy is. That decision would never be about him it would always be about her, and quite frankly I couldn't think of anything worse than something to do with her.

"Let's get back home?" I asked.

"Let's go sweetheart." He said and kissed my head before we walked home. The sun was beginning to come up, "would you look at this?" he said amazed, "there's always another day to start again Gabriella."

"I know." I said as we walked home. I know.

Chapter 28

"Right guys! Tonight, were going to the Venetian!" Euan was full of excitement as he locked his arm around Emily in the pool. "We've got some Gondolas to be going on!"

"The Venetian is meant to be really nice. Shall we do some gambling?" Paddy asked.

"Sounds like a plan!" David screeched. "But we definitely need some more drinks up in here Euan, get your money out!"

The last time I had visited Vegas I hadn't managed to go the Venetian. It was meant to beautiful, white stone and marble décor that reaches up to a hand painted ceiling that looks like the clouds in the sky. I wanted to go so badly before we came to Vegas. Still jilted by recent antics I didn't really have the energy to give half as much excitement for the rest of the group, but none the less it would be a nice evening.

"So? Shall we get dressed up girlies?" Emily smiled at Sophia and me.

"Of course, babe." I didn't even know what to wear, it was such a surreal feeling, I was here in body but my head is certainly not here. I couldn't help but still wonder where they are? They must've left Vegas in embarrassment. He must've tried to call me, surely, he wouldn't have left and not tried. Thankfully David had put that magical ban on his ability to contact on my phone, I think the term he used was blocking. But deep down, I hope he has, I hope he is as scared as me and knows this is an awful mistake. I wonder if I could ever take him back? What would happen to her? Could we delete her out of our life's or move away abroad and carry on like we were meant to?

"Gabby!" Sophia clicked her fingers in my face. "Get back in the room. Right guys One, two, three TEQUILA!!!!!!"

Jeez another tequila, although I feel nothing when it hits the bottom, so un Gabriella like. I should be passed out drunk by now. We all headed upstairs and began the daily getting ready routine, Sophia showered first, followed by me then finally David. David said he needed had more time to have a drink and not wait on Sophia caking my black panda eyes in makeup.

"Weet Whew ladies! Well you do scrub up well, I think I'm the luckiest guy in Vegas walking around with two sisters like you! Never mind sleeping in a bed with them both!" He cackled grabbing us both by the arm and heading to the foyer to meet everyone. To be fair we all did look great, everyone was put in 110% effort to enjoy every last minute of our time here. As we drove down the Vegas strip the lights glittered beside us. This place truly was one of the most magical places on earth. Every person we passed were smiling and laughing, there were street acts and flash cars, not to mention the most famous hotels we've heard of in our whole life's lining the boulevard beside us. The Venetian was so much better than the images online. It was one of the most luxurious hotels I've ever been in, the ceilings were bigger than I ever could imagine. Paddy squeezed my neck as we walked in. Euan and Emily strolled holding hands, whilst Sophia and David stood close looking at the Gondolas. The sinking feeling knowing Damian wasn't here came back, my stomach dropped as we got into the que and I couldn't help but realize this is too romantic and sweet to do at this point. Why was he not here?

"G? Coming on the boat with me?" Paddy asked.

"Paddy I can't I feel dizzy, I just want to wait. You guys go ahead" I said sitting down.

"No No No! You're coming with us and Paddy is going with David and Sophia. You're not missing this you're doing it with us ok?" Euan said sternly.

"I know, I know. I did want to do it, it just feels wrong that's all."

"Darling, I'd like to say something nice and heartfelt but let's be serious everything is wrong for you right now, but you're with us and that couldn't be more right."

We hopped onto the boat and after taking five hundred photos of Euan and Emily they managed to talk me into getting my solo photo on the Gondola. I never realized what the third wheel felt like until now. Solo photo on a romantic Gondola in one of the nicest hotels in the world, for fuck sake Gabby please do not cry.

"Should I get a pic with Gabby? Euan take a photo of us?" Here comes the sympathy shot, she's not alone she has friends photo. Everybody look a smile, great, she's natural at faking it. A couple of seconds later the Gondolier burst in to the most beautiful Italian song. His voice was sweet as sugar, and we all melted. It was literally above our heads, and as we were sailing past David, Sophia and Paddy as the gentleman started singing together. They were unbelievable.

"Do you guys know summertime sadness?" Paddy asked.

"Of-course we do! – I got th-"

And literally everyone around us burst into summertime sadness. David was standing up dancing and shouting at the top of his lungs whilst tourists passing by took photos. Where did Sophia actually find him? People looking over the river joined in and for a split second everyone forgot the drama and enjoyed the surreal moment we were currently living. The night carried on as we gambled and laughed and drank again and again. It was a little after 4am, and we had to sleep. Vegas 2014 was certainly going to be the death of me, and if anything, I definitely had that summertime sadness.

Chapter 29

I can't believe five days have passed and I haven't heard anything from him. I don't even know what I am going home to. What am I going to do? I was a grayish tanned and my eyes were like pandas, I had cried/mourned for five days, and now it was time to face the real reality - Home.

I stuffed the messy clothes lying on my packed suitcase I'd lived out of in David and Sophia's room. It was like I was stunned and it was happening in slow mo. I wish it was a dream.

"Gabby?" Sophia was behind me, "are you ok?" she said hugging me tight. "This is going to be the hard part, but don't worry you can sit with me, David and Paddy. We've all got you; it's going to be alright."

I was so fragile, and quiet I didn't want to speak, I didn't want to breathe. As if it wasn't humiliating enough I'll need to sit on the plane for eleven hours before the three-hour drive at the other side. It's time like this I wished we went to places like Barcelona. I miss Penny; I wonder if she'll even know her dads left us. God, I really need to stop crying.

Euan, Emily and Paddy met us in the foyer; I was shaking, hiding under my sunglasses.

"wee pal, only a little bit to go and you can see Penny and your mum. Don't worry about the next part, we're all here." Euan looked at me like he was going to cry himself. He knew me inside and out, the work dramas, the nights out, the laughs. Even the relationship he had with Damian is gone. I am so selfish for focusing on me and forgetting everyone has lost him.

"Euan? I want to go buy a hat before we go to the airport, will you come with me?" I asked.

"a hat? Em sure yeah ok, whatever you want. Why a hat?" he questioned me.

"I don't know if I'm gonna have a breakdown on this airplane and I don't want anyone to see my face. I can't wear sunglasses on the plane, can I? As if it's not bad enough already, people laughing at me." I jested.

"Well at least you're not gonna make us all look daft, moan lets go get you a hat, do you think you're a Kardashian or something? Koko?" he jested and hugged me as we walked into the mall near to the hotel.

Good plan G, get a hat and hide under up. Black tracksuit and black money team hat. Somehow it looked like id planned that outfit, thank god something is positive let's get to the airport. I'm gonna treat myself to a new a new handbag with that bonus. Breathe, breathe, breathe. I knew I could get through this, I'd already been through ten days of hell.

When we got in the taxi there was a sense of relief, everyone was positive and happy they left when they did as we still had an amazing five days, we managed to make the most of it. If it wasn't for these people around me I wonder what would've happened. Oh no here we go, tears again.

"Oi you! No more tears, we've got handbags to be buying!" Emily squeezed my shoulders smiling sympathetically. "Euan is letting me get one as moral support!" she smiled mouthing thank you behind him. She was such a sweetheart, such a lovely nature and Euan adored her. Why did that not happen to me? Why did Damian not want to do nice things for me?

Gabriella Johnstone stop it! Enough is enough. Pep talking didn't help much either. I just wanted home now. We drew up the airport and the boys got the bags, I felt weightless and tired, I needed a red bull, in fact I needed something stronger to get me through this flight.

"Gabby! Come off it, move, why are you standing there, we need to check in!" Sophia became like a mother. "you need to snap out of it, we need to get home. Emily, after check in take her for the handbag and we'll meet you at the bar for one last cheers."

My sister was like a superhero this holiday. We were so opposite but she held me together, fixed everything and made me feel safe. That was meant to be my job, I'm the big sister. If anything, her being here was a godsend. I can't believe I doubted it from the start.

Emily and I strolled towards the Michael Kors shop and decided to take our time deciding on all of the options. The shop was white and glossy, with gorgeous leather handbags positioned beautifully against the walls. I knew it had to be baby pink and pretty for Emily. But I wanted something more neutral and classy. I opted for a black, white and tan leather tote. At least I won't have to use that bag he bought me anymore. I was well on my way to deleting him out of my life. I was proud of myself and my efforts to re build everything he had broken, even though my bank balance was taking a pounding.

"I spent a bit more than I should have." Emily giggled, "Euan might be pissed but we need retail therapy and I am helping you by joining in." she looked at me for approval.

"of course, babe thank you." As we walked back to the guys, I looked down towards the bar down on the far left. "hey Emily, there's that Victoria's secret tracksuit I was going to buy – the dark purple one." I might have been seeing things, but I was pretty sure that it was Tilly and Damian. "Em . . . Emily its Damian and Tilly." I stopped dead and looked ahead of me. They were here in the airport, they hadn't left Vegas. They were holding hands and she was looking up at him adoringly twirling her ponytail. For a moment, everything in my world stopped. I had taken a bullet, so hard and so deep I couldn't feel a thing. I was gasping for air, I dropped my bag and luckily on my direct right there was a ladies' toilet. I started walking frantically towards the toilet before they could see me. "I . . . I . . . I need to go I'm sorry." And I walked straight to the bathroom. I ran straight into the cubicle put the toilet seat down sat down and locked the door. There wasn't enough air to breathe. How can they do this? What have I done to deserve this? Holy Fuck what the hell is wrong with these people! He was fucking lying in bed with me only five days before? Oh my god! I couldn't stop sobbing, they actually stayed here, I needed to call my mum, as I dialed the number I began to cry.

"Mum?" I sobbed.

"Gabby, what's wrong darling? Its 4am here? Everything alright?" she was still half asleep," what the hell is wrong honey?"

"Mum! They're here! Here as in walking in the airport all over each other here! What will I do? I bought this hat to hide and now I don't even want to get on the plane? What do I do?"

Before I even got a chance to finish, the door was being battered down.

"Gabby! OPEN THE FUCKING DOOR!" it was Sophia. I unlocked the door and sat with my head in my hands, she grabbed the phone and shaking her head she said, "you sit there a minute, Mum! I've got this handled, I'll call you back!" She clicked the phone down and grabbed me by the shoulders bringing me to my feet. She was red and angry, whilst I was broken and weak. What was she going to do?

"Listen to me and you listen right now! You have always told me that you were a strong and independent woman, yes?' She nodded at me. "well now is your opportunity to be it! We are in Las Vegas and if we do anything we are screwed! SO, YOU DO NOT LOOK AT THEM, DO NOT SPEAK TO THEM, AND ACT LIKE YOU DO NOT KNOW THEM!"

She was shaking and had a look of fear in her eyes. She brushed herself down and calmly spoke to me "Right, so now we know what is happening what do you want? We can get home and get on with this?" she smoothed down her outfit and started washing my face in the sink.

I couldn't speak for shock, although I wasn't sure if it was shock of them or Sophia's reaction. My heart was beating fast and hard and I couldn't hear anything but the pounding of the blood running through my body.

"Gabby?" she looked at me sternly.

". . . a double cheeseburger and two double vodkas." I couldn't even get the words out, I trembled as the she threw the water on my face.

"Emily, go and tell Euan to order it for her. We'll be down in five. I just want to make sure she's ok before we get out of this bathroom. Can you manage this Gabby?" I had no choice but to say yes.

"I think so." I mumbled.

"Ok well I think we can manage on that, come on let's go!"

The burger was hot and burned my lips. I wasn't even hungry anymore, I felt sick. The vodka as harsh on my throat. It felt like daggers were cutting through my neck but it was the only thing that could take the edge of the numbness. How was I going to get on this plane?

Paddy squeezed my hand as we stood in the que to board. I was drowning in the people around me. Numbness took over my body as I walked towards the lady checking our tickets. I couldn't make out faces only the shapes. I didn't want to get on this plane I wanted to scream and cry and probably tear Tilly's hair out, but everything was moving in slow motion.

"Gabriella?" Paddy said looking under my hat. "You ok petal?"

I gave a half smile, I was so scared to talk in case I screamed. When we got onto the plane we had four seats in the middle row, David and Sophia sat to my right and Paddy to the left. I was exhausted with the fear. I was going home to face my sad reality. we had made the most of our last five days but not one of us thought they would have the boldness to stay in Vegas.

I was glued to my seat, an eleven-hour flight with your ex-partner/love of your life six rows ahead sitting with your ex friend that sat beside you on the plane only ten days ago. This was a new feeling, I didn't even want to scream or cry. I wanted to disappear and for no one to ever find me again, I needed more Vodka.

I spent five days in my head going over and over the last few months and the changes in his behavior towards me. Does that mean he was with her that night after the pre-Vegas party? Or when Krystal was doing my hair? And when he went to Stirling for the car show? This had really happened? and what was I meant to do next was the biggest issue. I had to move back with my mum for the time being. Is there even a next? I had lost the love of my life to a cheap copy Gabriella. She had age and money on her side.

Maybe that was it. My head was spinning as they sat six or so rows in front of us on the plane. I couldn't interact with anyone I just wanted the plane to magically get home like Dorothy and the wizard of Oz.

"Sophia? She's not in the room man?" Paddy was worried sick. I could hear them talking but it was far away, I was in a bubble protecting myself from the harsh reality that was going back to Manchester with the potential for Tilly's mum to kick my head in on top of everything else.

"Gabby? Gabby? Gabriella? Excuse me!" Sophia said shaking me aggressively. "Get with it! We spoke about this, strong, independent woman. We can sort the rest out later. We just need to get through this flight. I'm not going to let anything happen to you. She won't come near you, if anything it's them who should be worried." Sophia had some serious attitude now, she was so motherly but at the same time the lightning bolt that was keeping me focused. Within half an hour, Sophia, David and Paddy were sleeping. I stared ahead at the monitor watching our Virgin plane cruised over the Atlantic.

It was such a final moment, he strutted down that airport with her without a care in the world, he had no respect or morals to show any remorse for the way he treated me and the way I was left. Not one phone call or message. He literally just left and had a five-day vacation with her. The worst part was I always said to Damian, never as a joke and never as a threat that if he wanted someone else he should just tell me so I could move forward. Not that I would have necessarily been happy but if he told me before we went to Manchester ten days ago I would have A. Took someone else to Vegas with me or B. Sacked the whole thing off and went to Dubai to think about what I wanted to do. But no, I got Option Z let's completely humiliate and embarrass you in front of all of our closest friends and push you to breaking point. To literally walk past you all hand in hand with your so called best friend. Tears rolled down my eyes once more, the tears kept on coming, it was like they never ran out.

"Come on darling, no need for that." Paddy put his arm around me and I hid my face in his shoulder. They were in front of us and I needed to pee. I walked to the back of the airplane and thanked god I bought this hat, no one could see my face and half of the plane were sleeping. I wonder if they saw me? Or if they even expected me to be there? Were they embarrassed?

Did they even take a second thought to consider the collateral damage they caused to my life, I suppose it was a hard one to tell, not even I knew how much damage they've caused.

Ten or so vodkas later I realized watching the other woman was not such a good idea. Sophia, David and Paddy all slept around me like a protective barrier. I couldn't say I wasn't grateful for them being so protective, I genuinely did appreciate every single bit. I was just so embarrassed that it happened in the first place. I had no choice but to sit on the plane and accept that my world has changed with no apology and no explanation. I needed to decide if I could handle being in our house, if I could ever look into his amazing blue eyes and not beg him to take it all back and be the person I know he is. But it had gone too far, he chose and I had no choice but to ride this storm, I could only control my reactions in front of them, everything else was up to him.

They stood five feet away from me when we collected our bags and came through passport control. I didn't even blink, or acknowledge their presence. They might have taken my world in one fell swoop but they were getting any tears from me. Arseholes.

I had to get home and get my stuff out of the house. Wait. Damian doesn't even have a key, he never took his house key. So only I have mine? Why would he not take his key if he knew that he was going to be sneaking off with her every other night? Wait? Did he not think he would get caught? Did they even plan it before? I don't want to see him, I don't think I can bear to look at him.

The magical blocking thing on my phone was amazing. Damian couldn't text, call or whatsapp. So how he would ever get the key from me I'll never know. I suppose it's not really my problem. Lesson learned, do not watch the other woman when the love of your life has just cheated on you with your so called best friend. It makes you want to do crazy shit. Speaking of crazy shit, I hope to fucking god I haven't washed and ironed his shirts for work. He can do them himself. I hadn't slept one wink on the flight home, but I've lost count of how many drinks I've had. I was completely shocked with emotion and alcohol. As we walked off the plane and Paddy put his arm around me and whispered in my ear. "Do not look at them, do not cry, do not laugh, and do not give them any satisfaction of your emotions. Be a brave girl. You've got this."

We stood in the que for our passports, unfortunately I had an old-style passport and had to wait in the slightly longer que. Sophia, David, Euan and Emily agreed to go in the faster que and collect the bags quicker if they were available, I looked at Paddy the whole time. I had no idea where they were but I was so scared to turn around in case they were near me. The que was long and It took nearly forty minutes to get through passport control. Once we cleared through to the baggage area Paddy escorted me towards the rest of the group. Four people down from us they stood waiting for their suitcases. I couldn't help but look. Damian looked straight ahead, but I knew he could see me. Did he feel anything? They collected their bags and walked off hand and hand.

That hurt like a knife in the chest. "Gabby, they were directly beside us but in the other que when we waited for the passport. Like not even a foot from your back. You did amazing." Euan gave me a hug as Paddy finished telling everyone what happened. "Sweetie, Emily and I will take you home, where do you want to go first?"

"I don't think it's fair for Paddy to drive home alone, you guys all have company and it did happen to him too. It just wouldn't be fair." I didn't have it in me to leave Paddy.

"Don't be silly Gabby, you relax in the back of the van." Paddy assured me. "you can sleep and have space, to you know. Prepare yourself."

"No, I can't I don't want to be that person. I'm going home in Paddy's car. End of." I couldn't do that, regardless of what help I needed, I couldn't leave Paddy behind. Especially when he had been so good to me. Sophia hugged me like she never wanted to let me go. "I'll see you at gran's ok. Follow us home please" David kissed my head, Euan and Emily squeezed me tight together. "You'll be ok princess. If you need us, then call us, anytime." Euan was the leader and the father figure of the group, what he said went, and I knew he didn't mind if I did call him anytime. It hadn't even happened yet but I knew that I would take him up on that offer, I'm not ok.

"I want to drive." I stated. Paddy looked flabbergasted, "Babe, you can't drive you've been drinking all day." he said concerned.

"I'm fine! Just let me drive it'll be ok, I need to get home now. I feel sick, I need to get my stuff from my house." Driving under the influence of alcohol in an uninsured car. Tempting fate at this point was probably not a good idea.

I sped the whole way home. I was going to my grans to shower and head to my house to get my things. I couldn't wait until tomorrow, delaying the process would only make it worse. I had travelled for around fourteen hours, hadn't slept or ate properly for days. But nothing was stopping this, I refused to prolong this anymore than it needs to be.

Paddy helped me with my suitcase as we stopped outside my grans house, my mum ran out of the door and grabbed me squeezing me so tight. "Are you ok darling?" she was crying too, "I have been so worried, are you ok? What's happening now? Do you need anything? Do you want a cup of tea?"

"She only drinks vodka now." Sophia chuckled at her back. " Is she ok?" Sophia gestured towards me looking at Paddy. This is when I realized that this is real. I didn't feel relived I felt scared, I was going to move out of our home today and it would be final. Seeing my mum made it worse, this was happening and I couldn't think of any other way to handle it.

"She'll survive, do you want me to stay?" Paddy asked my mum as he looked at me.

"We can take it from here. I'll message you later and let you know how you get on." I kissed him on the cheek. What a guy! Paddy had been left just as

I was, but he handled it so much better. I suppose they didn't live together and share bank accounts but they still spent two years together. That guy genuinely took care of me and tried to make me see the positive in the shithole that was currently my life. I would have to thank him some way, but right now I had to prepare to empty what was left of my old life.

"Mum, let's go and get my stuff from the house.' I said defiantly.

"When tonight? Are you not shattered darling? At Least have a cup of tea first?" She was so shocked by my behavior, I knew she didn't agree, but I just had to do this.

"Yes today. I'll have tea first." I showered whilst Sophia and David spoke about me and the situation. It was like it happened to someone else. I couldn't participate much in the conversation it was winding me up too much. Seeing my mum and my gran made it so much worse. I felt like someone had cut off my circulation and I was incapable of breathing. I couldn't listen to them talking about it again. It just too sad.

Before we left my grans house, Damian called my mum to ask for the key. She handled it perfectly, she explained I didn't want to be there when he was there and she would call him once we were finished getting my things. He was fuming.

As we pulled into the car park, my heart sank. My little car was waiting for me and the windows in the flat looked empty. I opened the door and my porcelain tiles that glistened in the sun did not look so shiny in the hallway. The flat felt lonely and cold, and the songs we sung to each other and memories we made felt like a distant memory. I sat on the floor looking at my wardrobe, I needed a minute to get myself together. How can I have the strength to do this? "Mum, can you sit with me for just a minute?" I sobbed into my hands. I didn't want to move out of our house. I didn't want to hand him on a plate to her, but I didn't have the strength to fight for someone that had already given up on me.

"Right my girl, the decision is in your hands. Do you want to pack up and leave right now, or do you want to get a few things and come back tomorrow, you don't need to rush anything? This is a lot to take." She sat on the floor and put her arm around me. "Even if you don't want to, you can do this girl. I know you can. You have the power to decide what you want right now. "She squeezed me and stood up looking into the wardrobe, she was overwhelmed. "Jesus Gabriella, look at these clothes, let's just come back tomorrow." She chuckled. "This is definitely a tough job!"

"No, let's do it now, I don't want to come back here." I opened all of the empty suitcases and began shifting my shoes and clothes into them, we had six suitcases so far, but it didn't even look like nearly enough. Damian had called my mum three times. But we didn't answer. The least he could do was give me some space.

"Gabby, he's calling again. Damian yes what is it? You want to come to the house and get your key? Well Gabriella wants to get her stuff without you being here, can you not give us some more time? I'll call you in an hour or so . . . yes, an hour. She wants to get her things together. Right Bye. . . Did you hear that, what do you want to do?" Mum looked uneasy and I just knew she wanted to scream for me.

"Why does he have to put this pressure on me, it's a fucking joke. He chose her! So, go and fucking stay at hers!" I was shaking with rage and tears! "It's a fucking joke!' I sobbed.

"I know darling but please don't swear, it doesn't suit you." Mum looked at me with that motherly stare. ". . .Although I don't think there are any other words for it!" she laughed. Swearing was the least of my worries. It was a joke; how could he do that then make demands off me like I'm being unreasonable.

I hadn't been into a bedroom yet, our bed was still as we left it, perfectly made on our silver grey crushed velvet high top bed with my hand picked satin Kylie bedding. I was such a twat, why did I spend so much money on bedding. Bedding didn't stop your man picking someone else. She probably didn't even have Kylie bedding in the first place, somehow it didn't feel like our bedroom anymore. It felt empty and strange, I wonder if she'd sleep on my side of the bed? The thought itself was sickening. I opened my underwear drawer and started piling all of nice pieces and sets into a bin bag. What did I need that anymore? Looking at the different out fits I pictured every memory we had, thinking of all of the hotels and good times we spent together. I immediately walked down stairs to the bin and chucked every last piece out. I didn't have time to worry about old used underwear, even if it cost a small fortune, the thought made my stomach turn. My mum was working her way through my makeup and hair boxes. Three pairs of straighteners, two hair dryers, four sets of rollers, one set of heated rollers. Over 100 nail polishes. I was a woman possessed. What did I even need all this shit for. "Mum whatever you think is crap throw out. We'll deal with it later." I had thrown out and packed up 50% of my Gabriella and Damian life and the phone rang.

"Damian, I told you we'd call you. . . your down stairs? . . . with Brendon? Well come and get your key. Tell Brendon to wait down stairs. He's coming up darling brave face. Be angry and remember what your grandad said think like a man." Mum walked into our en-suite bathroom and started emptying my toiletries. The hallway was lined start to finish with suitcases and bags. The house was a tip to be fair, the door opened and he looked at me sitting on the floor with my broken life scattered around me.

"What the fuck are you doing?" He snarled.

"Excuse me?" I was flabbergasted did he really just speak to me like that? "What the hell do you think I'm doing, I'm leaving. I think you made it pretty clear where you were standing earlier today."

"Gabriella, you don't have to do th-." I looked right at him.

"Do not ridicule me, I think you have done more than enough of that, you said you wanted your key. So, you can get it. I don't think there is anything else to say."

"Can you ask your mum to leave, I want to talk to you." his voice turned softer and I felt saddened by his tone. My mum heard him and quickly walked down stairs past him. For the first time in five days we were alone together. The room was filled with sadness, the last time we were together I threw his phone at him and left the hotel room. I never thought after that fight I'd be here confirming our split in our hallway. I continued packing but he didn't move from his spot in the doorway.

"Gabriella . . . Gabriella?. . I... I'm" he stuttered and stammered.

"Don't you dare fucking apologize to me to clear your conscience. How dare you fucking leave me at the other side of the world and strut around the airport with her like you had no idea who I was." I stood up staring at him, right in his eyes. His beautiful blue eyes were sad and he looked scared, for a moment I'd hoped he may even regretted it.

"Why did you have to take me there and do that! In fact don't answer that, you're a coward that's why, a fucking coward. You actually disgust me, look at you standing there in the Zara tracksuit I bought you, flaunting your new boxers I bought you in her hotel room! The saddest part about this whole thing is every single thing that you have on right now I bought you! What can you say that you did for me?" I was pointing to my new tracksuit and tiffany bracelet I had bought myself in Vegas. "Nothing, absolutely nothing! I never seen you as weak Damian. You were my hero, I loved you so much and you broke me, into a million pieces and walked away from the mess you made straight onto the next best thing." I tailed off, I had to hold back the tears. I couldn't cry in front of him. I couldn't have been any more honest with him if I tried.

"It's not what you think, all your fucking pals putting things in your head. You are all liars! Especially Euan and Sophia." He snapped.

"Is this some sort of a joke? Not one person has said one lie about you, you acted like a complete arsehole for weeks before we left. I ran around getting t shirts, buying fucking spinach so you could get into great shape for Vegas. Helped you maintain your gym schedule, took on all the responsibilities to make your life easier and I go to Vegas with you EVEN THOUGH I SAID I HAD A BAD FEELING!!!!!!!!!!! YOU DID THIS!!! YOU FUCKING DID THIS!!! THEN YOU TREATED ME LIKE SHIT FOR DAYS STAYING OUT ALL NIGHT OBVIOUSLY WITH HER, AND WHEN I QUESTIONED A MESSAGE I FOUND YOU LEFT. NO ONE SEEN YOU FOR FIVE DAYS AND WHEN WE GET TO THE AIRPORT YOU WERE HOLDING HER HAND. YOU"VE GOT TO BE KIDDING ME!"

"Gabriella don't shout, Brendan can hear you." he whispered.

"Hear me, I HOPE HE CAN FUCKING HEAR ME! How can he come and get you in Manchester? Did he know? Is it let's let everyone know except Gabriella for added effect, you knew what you were doing and I don't need any clarification, I know every time you seen her, spoke to her and every time you spent time with her before and during Vegas. I know your cardholder was in her room and you blamed me. I never did anything to hurt you, we have a life together, we have a home, we have Penny." tears filled my eyes but they never rolled down my cheeks. I didn't want to cry in front of him.

"Well you don't look that upset, you seem to be alright." He said cheekily.

"Alright? I would've walked to the town hall and married you in my pajamas. You were my partner and you broke it, you broke it so bad it can't ever go back. . . I want you to take your key and leave me to do what I need to do." I started packing my things again.

"Do you want me to help you with the bags?" he asked.

"Help me carry the bags out of our home, no, no thank you. I think I can handle that." This was becoming outrageous.

"But it's just you and your mum?" he questioned me.

"My uncle's will be here soon to help me." I retorted.

"Why do you need them to help you? What the fuck are you taking out of this house???" he started stomping around the house looking at furniture and shouting about what I can and can't take.

"Calm the hell down. I'll take everything I paid for. So, I'm sure you can figure it out." I snapped.

"Don't get fucking wide, this is my house as much as it's yours and I'm not leaving until I see what you're taking!!"

"I think you're wrong. The very least you owe me is the space to move out. I can't even bear to look at you, go to your girlfriend's house!"

Just as I said that our neighbour Michael came down stairs.

"Damian, Gabriella! How was Vegas, oh my god Gabriella, have you been shopping or what?" he stared at me and my suitcases layed out all over the hall. They were half packed, so it must've been hard to tell if I was packing or un packing.

Only we would argue with the front door open.

"It was good mate thanks." Damian said politely.

"And you Gabriella did you have a good time, Damian did you gamble?' he asked smiling at us.

"Em yeah a little bit." Damian replied.

"How much did you lose?" Michael asked.

"Everything." I replied. The look on Damian's face was priceless. He couldn't react, and I just had my first win in the ruin that was our non-existent relationship. The awkwardness was so obvious.

"Nice one guys, I'm going to the pub, catch you soon." And he walked down stairs fleeing the argument he didn't know he had interrupted.

"I think you should go." I said. "We don't have anything else to talk about.
"

"Gabriella, I didn't mean to-" he tried again.

"Don't! Damian please don't! Just leave. It's fine. The damage is done. I just want to get out of here." I shook my head and he turned and looked at me. Please don't say anything I prayed. I was so emotional and he was about to walk away from me. The world stopped and I looked at his eyes. The eyes that I have thought about every day since I met him. The eyes I thought our babies would have. I wanted to scream and tell him we could get through this, and that I didn't want him to leave. But I couldn't, it was over and as much as I love him it was just too far. He walked down the stairs as I continued packing. This is the hardest thing I have ever had to do.

My mum re appeared after a minute. "I couldn't even look at him. I called Brendon disgusting to his face too." I couldn't even reply to her. I just wanted this to be over with. She rambled on about Brendon and how Damian was a complete snake for acting the way he did. But I sat silent, I just needed my stuff, then we could go. Fifteen suitcases later, a table, a chair, a ginormous piece of art, a Range Rover, a pick-up truck and a Mercedes later. I'd packed up my life and in four hours I had had the last conversation with Damian and l walked away from the life I loved only ten days before.

"Mum, can you give me five minutes to say goodbye to the house?" a big part of me didn't want to leave.

"Of-course darling." she walked down stairs with my uncle and David.

I walked around stroking the surfaces and holding the pictures we had scattered across the window ledges. I sat on my dressing table chair and looked at my feature wall. She was going to use my things, and sit on my chair, this was my chair. I picked this chair, we chose that wallpaper. I wanted to pull the mirror off the wall. But I couldn't move. My gut instinct had become so strong I could feel when something was happening. The lead up to their decision I knew. I knew the whole time I just didn't want to admit he had the potential to be that person. My prince charming, my king, the man I loved destroyed me. I had no idea what was next for me. I had to go to work in two days. I don't know how I'll do it. The house didn't smell the way it usually did, it was as if when my feelings changed so did the house. It didn't fit me anymore, I didn't being there the way I used to.

I opened his wardrobe and there were no fresh shirts. I tipped them out of the washing basket and stuck the half-wet towels on top of them so they stank. He could learn to do his own washing, and I dipped his toothbrush in the toilet. That was for sleeping with me and her at the same time. Disgusting Rat. I never seen myself as a bitter woman, but I suppose it was the least I could do.

I closed and locked the front door for the last time and walked to the car. I sat in silence on the way home. We emptied everything into my grans garage. The worry on their faces was frightening, it was as if my grey depression had rubbed off on everyone else. I hugged my gran tightly and held Penny. Penny knew I was emotional, she kissed and licked my face. She would never see her dad again, I wonder if she even knew that?

When we finally got back to my mum's I sat on the couch. My brain wouldn't process the last 24 hours. I closed my eyes and tried to forget what happened.

"Do you want a glass of wine babes?" Mum asked.

"Yes please." I replied.

Chapter 30

It was the longest and second hardest day of my life. Second because saying good bye to my grandad (dad) would be hard to beat. The worst part about this is that, I didn't ever ask for this. I didn't ask for the showdown or the massive drama to end our what seemed so magical relationship. All I needed was some honesty. If he didn't want me he just had to say. I wonder what it felt like to be him right now? Did he have any idea what I was going through or did he just fall into her arms like I never happened?

A part of me was aware of the strength I had not to break in front of them/him. But I don't even know if that was the right thing to do. To be honest I didn't actually know what to do at the time. But if anything, I am pretty sure that this is going to come back to haunt me, I can just tell. Would I ever trust anyone again? How could I actually believe what anyone else had to say after that? How can I ever be in a place where I know the people in my life are genuine? Could I ever sit on an airplane again with my best friend? Do I blame him or her more?

 I actually hate him more for this than the actual cheating part. If there's one thing I know right now, its people are selfish and no matter what bus they have to throw you under, they will do anything to get what they want. The sad but true facts of life, and I Gabriella Johnson had just learned the hard way.

Seeing Marisa made everything more real. I didn't want to admit what happened. I didn't want to explain my lack of answers or lack of clarity. Marisa was my oldest friend from high school. She knew me inside out and if anything, this was embarrassing.

I knew she would be sad for me and I knew she would curse him. But I never ever wanted her to feel anger towards him. I watched her get out of the car and walk to my mum's front door.

"Babe, are you ok?" she hugged me tightly. "Well on the plus you've more the definitely hit your goal weight, you look good considering." She tailed off, I knew she was being overly nice and wanted me to feel like everything is normal. I had over cried and under slept and I did not need the sympathy vote right now. Maybe if I make her a cup of tea and give her some biscuits to choose from she'll forget the elephant in the room. She chose her biscuits and got comfortable on the couch.

"I'm so glad Sophia was there by the way. What would you have done without her, honestly such a lifesaver." She munched her biscuit. "And her? I mean what the fuck who even is she? A fucking wannabe? If that's his choice your best rid of that. The actual audacity of them both going along with it like that, it just doesn't even sound real, you couldn't make up a better sto- . . . Babe don't cry I'm just saying, this isn't on you, this is completely on them. You are the victim here. You are the one that doesn't need to apologize or back up anything that has been done. Although that face book was priceless. I'll get Sophia a drink for keeping it there later. right, this obviously isn't helping. But I did have a think, this is a really shit situation for you and I can't imagine how you are feeling, the only thing you can control is you. You can choose when to cry and when to laugh, who to pull or when to ignore your phone. What do you want Gabriella? What do you want for you?"

"Damian." I tucked my head in my knees.

'Ok, Damian I get that, but were going to take that option away for a minute and were going to think of other things. What do you want for you?"

"I want to breathe, I can't breathe at all. I feel like I'm suffocating, the pressure is just too much, I can't eat or sleep. I can't focus I just feel constantly sick. Everyone is looking at me like I'm broken, as if someone has died and I just can't handle it. I want to shout and scream, I just want to drive down the road and know I won't pass them, or go to work and not see his car on the motorway, or not have "our" friends messaging me like I have a disability, I just can' breathe Marisa, what can I do?"

"Right, were gonna come up with a plan so you can breathe. I've got you." Marisa was a great friend and we've never left each other's side since school. She was a part time artist, high school art teacher and soon to be Mrs Hobbs. She had been with Ryan since we were in high school. But she knows my ways and understands who I am and where I want to be. Strange thought when I don't even know where I want to be at this moment in time.

Chapter 31

"Pleeeeeeaaaaaassssseeeeee come to my mums wedding!!!!" Krystal begged.

"Babe, I don't think I can, it's just not something I think I'm up to it just yet." A fucking wedding? Is this a joke? I couldn't think of anything worse.

"Look babe, there's no pressure but we all want to spend time with you. Why not? It's only the evening event."

She was right, was I becoming the bitter girl who couldn't be happy for anyone else? Krystal's mum was widowed ten years before and finally met a man she wanted to spend her life with. How could I not be supportive?

When we arrived at the venue, Krystal looked stunning. She was so glamourous, I was guided across the dancefloor to our table. John gave me a massive hug and whispered, 'You're doing great G!" he rubbed my shoulder and gave me the look. The look that everyone gave me, the one that says you have just came out of a war and you look like you're holding on by a thread. Hanging by a thread looked like you were wearing a dress that is falling off you, caked in makeup because your eyes are so swollen and black, and hiding behind people to control your shaking. This wasn't about me, it was about Krystal's mum. Something inside me told me not to be selfish, and not to make this moment about me.

"Congratulations Moira! You look beautiful!" I said hugging her, "how was your day?"

"It was amazing gorgeous girl, you ok?" She said looking into my eyes.

"Of course." I nodded.

"I know you are girl.' She winked at me. And there it was . . . that song. My heart hit the floor.

Waves, it was on in every single place I knew. The most over played song of the summer, ringing round my head and cutting my heart to shreds. If only he knew what was happening, I hope he knew what he has done.

"Gabby!" Krystal's best friend Lulu was shaking me. "Wee not doing this here today. Let's make a new memory!" Lulu grabbed me and spun me around the dancefloor. I all of sudden felt light and to be honest I was a little bit embarrassed. How can I dance to this song? How can I re make such a horrible memory? The song he sung the full journey to London that weekend and here I am dancing with a friend of a friend pretending it's a different song.

"Gabby! Dance, this is our song, and this is about us having fun at Moira's wedding."

And she was right it was. Should I alienate myself of everything reminding me of them forever? Ok some things I could never do again. But I could still like the best song in the charts right now, couldn't I?

It would be the first time I'd stood on my own at an event not as Damian's girlfriend and it felt weirdly acceptable. I could make myself hold conversations with people and although there would be the strange please don't break down and cry conversations, people started to see me as me not as the addition to Damian's life. I was alone, and I certainly felt alone, but I have to say there is something weirdly warming about finally being your own person and not being an addition to someone else.

This was my first weekend off since, well, since the Vegas drama. So as promised I went to Krystal's mums wedding, took Penny out a walk and I promised the girls I've known since school I would go out tonight. Apparently, the best medicine is keeping yourself busy doing things you haven't done in years, which mainly involves drinking excessively and crying to your mum in the morning.

In all honesty, I'd neglected the girls from school for five years, I'd drowned myself in Damian's 'couple friends' and forgot about the Gabriella that liked to go out and socialize. We were going to our local pub Angels., going to Angels on a weekend meant that you would see everyone that you went to school with. I picked out a plain black dress and heels and caked on my makeup. Waterproof mascara was my savior these days. Drinking usually meant tears. But not tonight I had to learn how to compose myself and not to continually make an idiot of myself in public. Although not much time had passed and I am still convincing myself it is ok to be sad about this. People I knew were starting to believe I was having an actual breakdown, this was something I couldn't let happen. I need to repair my reputation.

"Gabby, don't be nervous you've been coming here your whole life, and if anything, everyone has your back. No one is against you." Marisa said.

Marisa, Jill and Laura were at school with me from day one. If I could handle facing my old classmates after I blasted my life over social media they are the team to have your back.

"I know I'm just nervous."

"Ok well don't be nervous, although Paul might be here. I'm just pre-warning you."

That's all I need, my crazy ex-boyfriend. The one before Damian that I have never spoken to since we broke up six years before. We had one of those toxics can't live with you can't live without you type of relationships. But it wasn't a clean break up and we have never spoke since. I wasn't really in the mood to say hi how are you after my life publicly fell apart. As, if it wasn't bad enough it not working out with the bad guy, guess what it doesn't work out with the good guy either. Cheers! My life is an actual joke.

We ordered our first bottle of prosecco and I downed my glass. I needed it. All the hello, how are you, the concerned sorry to hear what happened. Are you ok? You look skinny, you look well comments. I was going to need a buffer. I.E a lot of alcohol.

As the evening went on, the hellos and the sympathy hugs had started to wear out and we were free to dance. I managed to find Alan. Alan and I met in high school and were good friends. We sat beside each other in class and always had a laugh together. He was a safe bet, he wasn't feeling sorry for me or asking what happened. He bought me a jaeger and toasted to being single and alcoholics. It was the first time someone didn't pity me.

"You are a good one Gabby, but shit happens. We all get through it." He said as he ordered another round. The bar was loud and crowded. The younger generation of Uddingston Grammar started to fill our local. Who would've thought at twenty-five you could ever feel old.

"Gabby, can I talk to you for a minute?" someone tapped me on the shoulder. Fuck! It was Paul.

"em, yeah sure. What's up?" I said casually.

"look, I heard what happened and I'm sorry. I really didn't think we'd ever see each other again never mind have a conversation. I really thought when you met him that was it for you. He was the one. I'm sorry I tried to stop it from happening in the beginning. I was just possessive over you, I didn't want anyone else to have you even if I couldn't. . ."

"Don't be silly Paul. It happens, life just moves us on. You don't need to worry about it. Were cool."

The honest truth was we were not cool. He was a sociopath, but It was easier to forgive and forget than bring more drama to my life. Paul made me feel insecure and shaky, he always said no one would ever want me except him. And here I am six years later standing in our local royally dumped proving him correct.

"Anyway Paul, I'm glad you're doing well. Enjoy your night." I said and turned back to Alan. Luckily, he'd ordered us two vodkas to keep us going.

"To moving on!" he toasted.

"yeah moving on." I gulped my drink and took a breath. No tears Gabriella, I promised not tonight. No tears, no more embarrassing moments.

"do you think it's me? Am I too much?" I asked Alan, he drank his drink and didn't respond. "Do I want too much? Do I need too much? I only want to have a great life and work hard and enjoy building it. Is that wrong?"

"Gabby, it's not wrong just some people can't keep up with you, and that's a good thing too. You just need to dust yourself off and know you're better than all of this and everything that happened. It's hard but you'll get by.

You're not too much, you're just enough – always remember that."

"Can I have tequila? I feel like I need a boost?"

"Sure, G whatever you want. Two tequilas please?"

we necked them together and I couldn't help but lean on his shoulder.

"Alan, do you know what I really need. Like really really?" He looked at me confused.

"I just want someone to hold me, and not let me go."

"Right G, time for home. Sorry Alan, this is all new to her." Marisa said escorting me into a taxi, I meant every word. I just want a cuddle. Someone to pick up all of the broken pieces and stick me back together." In my drunken mess the worst part about this was I meant every single word. The only way to deal with this is to stay silent and pretend you didn't just say that.

"Did you hear Gabby?" Marisa cackled "I need someone to hold me? What's she like? We'll hold you hun, just don't ask random guys we went to school with that. Ok? Let's get her to bed. We've got a long way to go with this one."

The taxi journey was short and quiet. Part of me was embarrassed but the other part knew I needed help, I was broken into so many pieces how would I ever go back together if I couldn't find someone to help me?

Chapter 32

It was easy, get home from work and relax, who cares if Damian has moved into the house Tilly's dad built for her. It's no big deal, at least she wasn't lying in my bed anymore. I am so tired of hearing this shit. Can I just be left to get on with it? Why does everyone feel the need to go on about them, I know, I actually know he is with her, I actually know she was sleeping in my bed, I actually know they told everyone it never happened till after. I actually FUCKING ALREADY KNOW!!!! Gabriella calm down, you need to compose yourself. Just go home, see Penny and have a glass of wine, there's nothing better than that. All I had to do was keep telling myself it's fine, everything's fine. Like so fine. Maybe I should put on the radio and chill, Radio one will do. Shake it off! Shake it off! - seriously fuck that, I had to skip that shit. I cannot shake off anymore. I put the I G G Y , put my name in bold, I been working, I'm up in here with some change to throw. I'm so fancy, you already knowwww - I love this song. Even if that stupid bitch copied my ringtone. It was my favorite song first. I'm in the fast lane, from LA to Tokyo. I just had to tell myself, you can't hate everything you loved because of her - I mean them. So, what she liked a song you liked and made her ringtone the same as yours. It took a minute to gather my thoughts and actually calm down. No more Gabriella, no more crying or worrying no more getting upset. You are who you are. This was starting to get out of hand.

"Gabriella, are you on your way home?" mum asked.

"Yeah, I'm ten minutes away." I replied

"Ok, I'll put the dinner on, shall we go a walk tonight? You know instead of having a glass of wine straight away?" she chuckled.

"Yeah ok, is Penny ok?"

"She's great, see you soon darling."

'See you soon mum"

At least I had my mum to go home too, a walk before wine, hmmmm maybe it's the beginning of a new me. Or maybe I just shouldn't lie in the house every night. FUCK SAKE Gabriella. What the hell is wrong with you!!!!

And there I was at the barrier of my old flats car park. With no fob and no key. Complete autopilot. Why do I still think I live here? I trembled whilst I dialed mum. "Mum . . . I've only went and drove to the flat haven't I?"

"Awww Gabby, what you like silly girl." she laughed.

"It's not funny mum! It's my house, I live there, I built that house, my wardrobes are there!!"

"Please don't cry, you need to calm down. It's just a silly mistake, Gabby? Please breathe and calm down. It's not the end of the world."

"Mum it is the fucking end of the world!!!!! She stole my fucking ringtone!!! I'M STILL HER FACEBOOK PICTURE!!! THIS IS TORTURE!!!!"

"Your what? And your what?"

"MY FUCKING RINGTONE AND Y FUCKING PICTURE!!! SHE WON'T LET ME GO!"

"Gabby, what are you on about? Can you just come home? We don't need to go the walk if you don't want to?"

"I don't care about a fucking walk, everything I do I am back to square one, or square minus 5 million. She took my ringtone! She want's me on her Facebook, She took my hair! She took my personal trainer, she took my boyfriend, she took my house!!! She took fucking everything!!!! AND NOW IM OUTSIDE THE PLACE I USED TO FUCKING LIVE WITHOUT A KEY CRYING LIKE AN IDIOT!!!!!!"

"Ok . . . don't cry. I know it's awful darling, but please turn around and come home. What if someone sees you there?"

I looked and no one was in our spaces - sorry their spaces. How could I be so stupid, god what if he sees me, I better go!

"Right, ok. I just need to catch my breath and I'll come home."

"Good girl, we'll have a wine and no walk ok?"

"Ok mum" I clicked the phone and decided to drive home. I've genuinely lost my mind.

The what seemed like fantastic once in a lifetime opportunity that I was so grateful for, is now so hard, almost unbearable, no one understands me, I can't even get through a meet and greet with a customer never mind close a deal. It was a joke. The boys were enjoying it to be fair. "Princess is falling off her pedestal!!!" It was frustrating being so in adequate. I always worked well, I always knew what to do, but I just couldn't focus.

Sunday afternoon pouring with rain, I had zero chance of selling a car. Eleven days have passed and I'm starting to worry. Between my daily breakdowns, inability to communicate effectively and lack of customer appreciation I was surely walking on thin ice. Damian Mclaughlin ruined me, and soon to be my career.

"Guys!! Sales call!" the receptionist shouted through.

"It's mine!!" I said grabbing the phone. "Hi, you're through to Gabriella at Porsche Glasgow. . . yes . . . sure. . . yes, can I take your name? and mobile number? And finally, your email address sir? Perfect. Ok so if we can do that are you in a position to pay a deposit over the phone? Ok great. As it is Sunday the manager I need to speak to is not in the showroom I will need to give him a call and call you back is that ok? . . . perfect. I will call you right back, thank you for your enquiry."

Finally, something I can work with. It was a straight shot. Well sort of, he wanted £1000 off a pre-owned Cayman S 2013. All I had to do was ask Raymond and then go from there.

"Hi Raymond, I know you're not in the showroom, but I have a hot lead. It's for the 2013 Cayman S upstairs. The man is calling from Leeds. He said if we take £1000 off it he will buy it?"

"Ok darling. I don't want to do this, but seeing as you've not had any luck recently we'll do it and hopefully it'll get you back on a roll. Take the deal and I'll see you in the morning." Raymond wanted me to do this more than

I did, I couldn't let him down.

It was 16.10pm in the afternoon we had just closed the showroom. Scott and Sean were finishing up as I made the last call. Scott was dropping me home as we now took turns on the Sunday run as one or both of us would take it too far on a Saturday night, although recently it seemed to be him taking care of me.

"Hi sir, It's Gabriella calling from Porsche Glasgow. I am calling as I have now spoke to my manager and he said if you are able to place a deposit just now over the phone we will honor the £1000 contribution. . .. Oh, so you want to speak to your wife? Ok and when would you be looking to make a decision? Tomorrow morning? Sure, no problem. Well please give us a call when you have spoken to her and we can go from there. Thank you enjoy your evening."

"Gabby!! don't cry!!" Scott hugged me. "It's alright it's just a bit of bad luck, nothing else. Things will start to look up soon, I promise."

"Bad luck? Seriously? Bad luck Damian fucked off and took my house, and my sanity oh and wait my confidence in my fucking job! Is this a joke?"

"babe come on, just calm down, it's Sunday night we can all relax. You'll get the deal in the morning it'll be fine." Sean piped up.

"there is nothing fine about anything anymore. I don't even know how this is even a thing! My life is a grade A disaster!"

"Right you! That's enough just calm-"

"Wait! What is that?" I asked.

"what is what wee yin?" Scott answered.

You're still the one that I love, the only one I dream of the only one I kiss god night. You're still the one I run too, the one I belong to.

"my life is the fucking Truman show!"

"wo wo wo! Little one, don't cry it's ok, honestly, it's fine. You don't need to cry. Sean ?? what we gonna do? I mean this song right now?" Scott laughed and hugged me at the same time.

"take her home, she needs her dinner and her mum. It's alright-" he chuckled. "it's coincidence, and to be fair a good a song."

"Shut up Sean!" my life seriously can't get any lower. "Please can you just take me home Scott, I'm done."

"let's go shorty." He said as we walked to the car.

I've never hated myself as much as I do at this moment. I have no Damian, no house, been completely humiliated, I can't do my work without failing and I can't keep my cool when I listen to the radio. We drove in silence down the motorway. I thought it was best to look out the window and act like I wasn't crying.

"Listen wee yin, if you don't stop crying I'm gonna have to chuck you out the car!"

I couldn't figure out if he was serious. "seriously?" I chuckled wiping my face. "What would I do without you brother?" I asked.

"the wife's gonna kill me for saying that to you. But I just love ye, and I hate seeing you like this. I wish I could do something? Should I batter him?" he laughed.

"Nah, waste of time. Plus, it's not nice to hit girls." We laughed and for a second I remembered I can still laugh even though it's an awful time. Thank god Scott is in my life on a daily basis, I don't think I'd know what to do in the showroom if I wasn't making him coffee. Shania Twain I once loved you, but why today?

Chapter 33

As if Shania didn't ruin your life enough, have you ever listened to Beyoncé and felt like she sung every single word about your life? I couldn't shut her songs out of my head, but at the same time listening to music is the only thing that is giving me any space from this current hell. It felt like I was running out of tears, I'm so angry and upset I can't even cry anymore. Does that mean I'm over it? A long time ago I used to sing. I wasn't too bad at it actually but when my grandad passed away I just lost the urge to do it publicly, it was our thing. He'd take me out three times a week so I could sing in pubs across Glasgow. It was my party trick, my getting approval from the older generation and it made me feel great, it was like every emotion I had I could use it to release my stress. My current favorite was resentment, it was years old but a classic that would never die and be used for women to zone out for years to come when they faced the same heartbreak as our hero Beyoncé.

It was another Saturday night in chilling with my mum and her best friend. The weekends were starting to get repetitive, I would be asked if I am ok and how I'm feeling. I'd cry for half an hour and we would drink wine and talk about how we hope life would turn around for us one day.

"Mum, I've been practicing a song."

"A song? What when? I haven't heard you?"

"Just in the car and stuff, I feel like I need to get it out and I haven't done this for ages. I want you to hear it."

'Well Auntie Zara wants to hear it too, wait till she comes out of the bathroom."

I grabbed a glass of water to wash away the wine I'd just downed. I just wanted them to hear how I felt. I needed to get it out and get it over with.

"Are we getting a song?" Zara was excited and perched herself on the end of the sofa eager to hear what I had to sing. I wasn't nervous but the sad feeling I had come over me. I didn't want to cry, I mean come on it's only a song.

As it came to an end auntie Zara left the living room she was in consolable. I had never seen her like that in my life. ". . . Mum is she ok?"

"She'll be fine honey. That was really amazing babes. I'm so proud of you, please don't ever forget your talent." She wiped the tears from her eyes and auntie Zara came back into the room.

"Gabriella, I genuinely felt every single word you have just sang. He is an absolute bastard just like the rest of them. I wish I had the strength to do what you've done."

Auntie Zara had lived under a cloud of the unknown for more than twenty years. I could see the sadness in her eyes. How do we know what is right? Leaving? Staying? Fighting for the love of your life? Or fighting for your own happiness? Should you shout from the rooftops about how happy or sad you are? Or should you make the decision to walk away and not try at all? Who was right? Millions of people all over the world suffered relationship breakdowns and break ups every day. What gives me the right to be angry and upset every day? What gives me the right to fail at my job because I allowed someone to shatter my confidence?

I suppose there are too many external factors consider when your life breaks down. But I didn't want to be the girl that settled for an ex council house and a husband that leaves on a Friday and comes back on a Sunday. I wanted the magic, I want someone to grow beside me that wants to enjoy every moment and plan our future lives together. I wanted Damian to be that person. I don't want to sit in on a Saturday night with my mum singing songs about how heartbroken I am. I need to change this, thinking about auntie Zara made me feel sad by her reaction. Does every woman in the world feel like this? That men are always going to choose someone else? or do we hold on and hope that they may come back to us? Whatever the reason, people make mistakes but should those mistakes haunt the people that have been affected forever? Is this what will happen to me? I'll cry randomly because they ran off together and left me with nothing. All because I heard a song that is screaming how I feel? It wasn't until now I realized how dangerous it can be to be so dependent on one person. Is it ok to give someone the right to control your future and your feelings?

I don't think I can do this to myself. It can't be that hard to find someone else worthy of my love. Surely someone will not take advantage the way did? Or will I end up living alone and adopting Chihuahuas for the rest of my life? Either way I need to look at this situation and realize that I can't live under someone else's control. I need to be able to do things for myself, the issue is how do I actually do that?

Chapter 34

I had to tell Raymond how I was feeling, I couldn't breathe. The only place I felt safe was in Porsche. I'm losing my mind, I can't even get any hair done without hearing the latest news update on how happy they are. I struggled in the gym in case I seen them. It had to stop, I had to man up and tell Raymond my thoughts.

I walked into the glass office and held my head, "Raymond, do you have a minute?" he looked up from his desk and closed his laptop.

"For you anytime darling, you ok?" he asked.

"Raymond, I need to tell you something." The tears started rolling down my cheeks.

"Don't cry darling what's happened now?" he passed me a tissue.

"I can't do it anymore. . ."

"Can't do what?' he seemed confused.

"I can't be in Glasgow anymore, I can't breathe. I can't go anywhere without hearing about them, or seeing him driving to work or to the hairdressers or my personal trainer or nothing. It's just getting too much. I think . . . I think I'm going to resign . . . and it's nothing to do with you or the boys. . . It's how I feel." I paused. He looked so upset with me.

"Darling don't be so stupid. Damian has been an absolute idiot and we all love you so much, the team wouldn't be the same without you, why don't you move to the other side of Glasgow and just change things, hairdresser etc. That'll help surely." he passed me another tissue.

"Raymond, the only time I feel safe is when I'm here. You guys are like family to me, and in all my years in Mercedes I never felt as close to that team as I do you guys, I could never thank you enough for all the help and support you have given me, especially since I have come back from Vegas."

"Gabriella, don't throw away your career too. I know you're hurting and I know how hard it has been for you, I can see it in your face. But changing brand won't change anything, surrounding yourself with people who don't know you won't give you the support you need at this time. Trust me, just bide your time and by this time next year you'll be laughing. You're the next business manager and you're the youngest team member not mention the only female. Do you know how amazing that is?"

"I really do, and that's what's making this so much worse. I want this career and I want to use my potential but I've lost it. I don't feel like the girl I was before, I feel broken and in capable, and I would never be disloyal to you and go to another dealership. It will never be as good as here. I . . . I . . . want to move to Dubai."

"Dubai???? Why? To live in a desert where women are second class? And Arabs are rude to you? You can't drink? And there is no one there? You need people around you darling and that is not the place for you, you don't need to be so extreme. If you want time off a month, two months whatever I can arrange that for you. Whatever you need but you don't need to that." He seemed shocked. But I did need this, I wasn't sure how long it would take or what I actually needed to heal, I just needed to go, living here was exhausting, I have nothing left, I want to breathe.

"I am so sorry for saying this to you, and I know you would never give me bad advice. I'm not handing you my resignation or finalizing everything. I just appreciate all of your time and care for me and I want you to know exactly where my head's at. I really do care about this place and everyone in it. I just don't feel like I don't measure up anymore. I can't even organize a delivery; my head is so scrambled." Raymond put his arm around me and wiped my tears.

"Right, no more tears Gabby, don't be silly. We can help you through this, whatever it takes. Don't make any rash decisions. You're safe here." he hugged me tight. "Right go and wash your face you've got motors to sell, don't let them take this too. Clark!! Get this princess a tea! Two sugars! she needs it." he shouted through to the sales office.

"I'm onto it Ray!! Little dafty!" he said as I walked past. "You're going nowhere. Were family."

Knowing we were a family made it worse. I had no idea where I was going or what I can achieve in Dubai. I just don't want to be here anymore. I can't drive past my old home knowing that they were together, lying in my bed, in my sheets. Drinking from my cups and parking in my space. The thought made me feel sick, how could I live a normal life with them flaunting themselves everywhere I go and everywhere around me? It was just too much to bear. I would apply for jobs and see if I can get the strength to actually do it. I genuinely have nothing to lose, someone already took it.

A couple of days later, I officially resigned and Raymond accepted. He understood my point of view and backed my decision. He said as long as I was Gabriella Johnson I was welcome back in Porsche Glasgow anytime. For being so unlucky I was certainly lucky in some other aspects of life. I just needed to sort out how I would survive in Dubai. Operation go get a job commenced.

Chapter 35

Meeting Lottie was strange, it was like meeting someone you already knew but you hadn't actually met them before. She was Blonde and petite bit with a Kim Kardashian bottom. We hit it off straight away Lottie's husband had been caught red handed with his PA right before Lottie packed her suitcase to come to Dubai. The one difference was she left with the promise he would join her in six months, sadly eight months have passed and no sign of the husband, Lottie moved out and she moved in. Lottie was a nurse and needed a roommate for her small two-bedroom apartment. Luckily for me, I needed a place to stay and Lottie's heart was just a broken as mine. At least we could watch Bridget Jones and cry together.

I had to look for work and then look for peace of mind. I knew I was good at selling cars, and regardless of my recent performance I deep down hoped that everyone understood it was the circumstance. I could do bar work? or work as a PA, but deep down I knew my strengths and why change everything? Was changing the country you live in not enough?

Lottie stayed in an apartment hotel in JLT, not the holiday Dubai I was used to with five star facilities and people waiting on you hand and foot. I had little money and little experience on the living on the other side of the world front, but her place was small and homely. It was full patterned blankets, and Kath kitson accessories, nothing like the simple and classic style that had flowed through my old place with Damian. There were pictures on the walls of family members and nights with the girls, stuffed animal toys from past relationships and quotes about positivity and looking forward. I don't even know if this is what I need, but I'd much rather be here there staying somewhere else on my own.

My first interview was with Mercedes Benz on Sheikh Zayed road. I squirmed walking into the showroom, it was huge and I was tiny, my heels echoed my presence as I walked to the reception desk.

"Excuse me. . .em hi, my name is Gabriella and I have an interview with Mr. Ahmed. He . . . em he asked me to be here for 10am." It was 9.30am, but I didn't know where I was going.

"Hi Mam, my apologies he does not start till 11am, would you like to come back?" the receptionist questioned.

"Can I wait?" I answered.

"Of course, would you like tea or coffee?"

"No thank you, Can I walk around for a while?"

"Of-course mam."

The showroom was beautiful, the cars were immaculate and there were staff every ten feet. Everyone greeted me and smiled. I wasn't used to seeing so many different people from different places before. But for some reason I didn't feel scared. I could work in a showroom like this. They had G wagons and S 500s and AMG cars scattered across the showroom. This place meant business and I could feel it.

Mr. Ahmed arrived and my palms began to sweat, he questioned me on my knowledge, experience and charisma. He questioned my purpose in Dubai, my purpose in Dubai what a great question? I got cheated on by the love of my life and my fake best friend, and I am currently running as far away as humanly possible so I can breathe, I don't want to see them or hear about them or explain how I'm am ok despite reports of how insanely happy they are, and also not to mention that I can barely string a sentence together because my mind is so fucked by this horrible situation. That is probably not a good idea so stick to the politically correct answer Gabby.

"We'll I've actually been coming to Dubai since 2008 with my grandparents and it's a place I have always wanted to live. Recently my life changed a little and I now have the opportunity to go for my dream." I smile and smise with my eyes. (I knew watching America's next top model for years would eventually come in handy.)

Mr. Ahmed thanked me for my time and congratulated me on the interview and asked if I would be happy to proceed to the next step which was meeting the General Manager David in their Diera branch. Diera? Where was that? Eager to bag myself a new job I agreed and asked for directions to Diera. Mr. Ahmed called a driver and he took me there. It was over thirty minutes away in a more Arabic area. This was a whole new Dubai experience and it has only been two days.

The place was fascinating, there was people everywhere and the streets bustled with business. I walked into the next showroom and found David. He was British and had worked for the company for a long time. He explained the ins and outs of the company and the level of person they were looking for. The standards were high, but pre-Vegas Gabriella was more than fit to do the job. I was grateful at the effort the company went for me today and I hoped for the best. I crossed everything and went back to the apartment. Waiting for Lottie was boring, I suppose I'd never been on my own to know what it was like.

"Motormouth!" Lottie laughed. "can you calm down, they've not called you yet. Just take your time and keep trying until you know. We have just under three weeks and I know you'll get exactly where you want to be. Love you babe, now get some sleep. It's only just begun." She began to close my door and blew me a kiss. "We got this girl!"

"Good night Lottie." I closed my eyes hoping I'd drift into a deep sleep, but I was too excited and anxious. I had no clue about what happened today and I have no idea where we are. But all I know is when I wake up tomorrow I can breathe, and they are not near me. The thought alone calmed my fragile bones and ushered me into a deep sleep.

We had a little less than three weeks and every day I walked in and out of the showrooms I had shortlisted. Mclaren, Aston Martin, Mercedes, BMW,

Porsche, Ferrari, Maserati and a real estate company - just in case. The only people hiring were Mercedes, Porsche, Mclaren and the real estate company.

I had never done real estate before, but as my Dad says selling was selling. The gentleman I met was friendly and confident. He made me believe I was the best real estate salesman in Dubai. I hadn't even viewed a property never mind try to sell one to someone. But my gut told me as prosperous and exciting as this job was I don't think I can change my career completely. I needed some sort of security, and selling cars would be the security that would get me through. At least I knew my craft.

As Mercedes had offered me the job they said HR would contact me to sign the contracts. By the time this offer came through I was in talks with Mclaren and Porsche. I had a soft spot for Mercedes as I learned everything I know there, from the basics of speaking to people, to using open questions and closing the customers. I agreed to sign the papers once HR contacted me. But in my mind, this was a backup, I had moved onto Porsche back home and the difference in the customers and the level expected was much higher than Mercedes. Surely, If there was a time to grow, it had to be now?

Porsche was a phenomenal place to work. Our Glasgow branch literally blew me away, every single detail was carefully planned and executed. The passion of the people and the brand made every day work interesting. But Mclaren? Could I Gabriella Johnson go to Dubai and work for Mclaren and rocket myself into the top end prestige cars and show everyone what I'm really made of? Hell yeah! What else could possibly go wrong.

"Hi Darling, how is it going over there?" My dad asked.

"It's pretty good, I mean we are living in old school Dubai where no one around us really understands us but it's definitely a learning curve." I replied.

"and what about the job?"

"well, I have some options, the real estate company said yes, and I really want to do it, but I just feel like it is a massive risk to come here to go to a job I don't know or understand and it's commission only. So that's no, Mercedes offered two weeks after they confirmed at my interview but I feel like I was a bit forgotten about. So, it just leaves Porsche and Mclaren?"

"Wow! Not bad choices darling, I don't want to make a choice for you but I think you need to think about where you will get the most exposure to the customers, remember you are new to the country."

"yeah, yeah I know dad. But could you imagine I sign a contract with Mclaren? It's so not Glasgow? And it's amazing. Surely I can do it?"

"you can do anything you want, but I want you to sleep on it and when you wake up you'll know what to do. I've got to go to a meeting but call me tomorrow. Love you."

"Love you dad."

The thought of this actually happening is baffling. Julia was already in bed sleeping for work and I climbed in beside her and fell asleep.

When I woke I felt something change? Mclaren was a phenomenal opportunity, but how many McLaren's could you sell in comparison to Porsche? Without talking exact numbers, definitely not as many. I showered and dressed and headed to the Porsche head office on Sheikh Zayed Road. Beside me was the new showroom in progress and near completion. It was towered above me, three floors which would showcase sixty cars at any time. Two basement floors, a twenty-bay service department and a rooftop terrace for events. This was my new castle, I had to make this work no matter how hard or how much I will miss Porsche back in Glasgow. All I have to remember is every day I can breathe, because they won't ever be in my place.

I handed over my Ids and signed my contract. I would be back on the 27th of December to start my new life. I couldn't help but feel a pang of sadness that Damian isn't sharing this with me, he would've loved this opportunity. I wanted to call him and tell him he's made a mistake, and that he could have this with me. That we can still do everything we ever said we wanted to do and that it was ok. I began to type in his number and stopped. Why would he want to hear from me, he picked another life with her? Get on with it Gabriella, he didn't want you. I genuinely hated this voice I had in my head these days.

"OHHHHH MYYYY GOOOODDDDDD!!!!! I can't believe you done it!! All we need to do is go home and get the rest of our stuff and we can start again. I'll have a nap then we can go out and celebrate!! Wake me up in an hour!" Lottie giggled walking into the bedroom.

"Ok babes, I'm gonna skype Euan and tell him the news."

"K babes, Good Night! Love you!"

"Hiya pal!!" Euan chirped.

"have you got time??? I have so much news!" I genuinely couldn't wait to tell him.

"How is it over there? I'm just chilling had the Christmas party last night!"

"Aww amazing, well tell me about it in a minute!! You are speaking to Gabriella Johnston Sales consultant for none other than Porsche Dubai. The soon to be biggest showroom in the world!!!!"

"Holy shit pal! You signed the contract? That's amazing"

"Yup! Sure did, after thinking about everything it was the best option. I've had a year with Porsche and I don't know enough about the company yet, I'll miss the boys in Glasgow that's a guarantee but I need to breathe."

"You're better off without darling. You remember that girl that worked in reception in Giffnock? The pretty one?"

"The fake tanned one? I don't like her? Why?"

"why don't you like her?" he questioned me.

"She kept looking at me whenever I was in the showroom, I just felt like her eyes were constantly on me? I was just Damians girlfriend bringing in Penny and his lunch the odd occasion what was the big deal? She was a complete weirdo!"

"hmmm that's interesting because last night she told everyone she had a thing with Damian for a few months before you both broke up?"

I put the ipad down and sat on the sofa. Breathe Gabriella breathe. Not again, why is my life such a farse? Everything I thought I had was a complete lie. A complete and utter lie.

"Gabby! Gabby! Come on? I wouldn't tell you if I thought it would hurt you, I'm just relaying what was said, lift the ipad, I want to see your face." Euan stuttered.

I couldn't move, my heart wrenched, this was real. So, real, everything we ever had was a lie.

"Gabby!!! Come on now!" Euan yelled at me.

"I just need a minute." I wiped my tears and took a deep breathe.

"Darling, at least it's not your problem anymore. It's who he is and to be fair it looked like she wanted her fair share of the drama."

"As if it wasn't dramatic enough." I sniffed.

"You go out and enjoy your night! You just bagged the job of a lifetime in your favorite country in the world with no help from anyone. He just couldn't keep it in his pants . . .again" he laughed.

"It's not actually funny Euan, but on a serious note how did I never see it?"

"because you were in love with darling, and that's ok."

"not really when I have been completely humiliated, not only in Vegas. Oh god!!! They must've all been laughing at me in that showroom. There's me taking in his lunch on my day off, and picking him up after nights out. They must've known and thought I was a complete idiot. Euan why did i-"

"Gabby Shush!!! You did because you loved him and it was real for you. Don't get upset that there's another one. Be happy because it means she doesn't have anything any more special than anyone else. He just got caught and had to lie in the bed he made for himself. If anything, he humiliated himself. I thought we could stay civil for work purposes but it turns out he's too good for us all now. I know you've lost out, but we all have. No one will grieve more than you wee yin, but I promise you – no one can do what you've just done after that. So, dry your eyes and get yourself out to celebrate!"

"I can't Euan, how can I not know this? I'm such an idiot. As I if it couldn't get any worse."

"Well it could, you could be at home living with your mum, going out to the same places you've went your whole life, but you're in Dubai. You've just signed a contract to work in the biggest Porsche showroom in the world and start a life you've spoke about for years. You might not have Damian but you certainly don't need his balls to help you get what you want!"

"Euan!!!" I can't help but laugh. "Ok, I'm not 100% but I'll go have a drink for your great speech."

"Darling? Just remember. Leopards can never be tigers! Love you!"

"Love you pal, and thank you. I'll send you some pictures later."

Leopards can never be tigers, how true a statement. Here I was in an apart hotel after signing my new contract and getting ready to go out and celebrate in Dubai. Do I care? Should I care? Probably but I shouldn't let it stop me. I achieved this on my own, and I should be proud of that.

Chapter 36

"Soooo, Princess Porsche!!! Now we have a permanent set up in Dubai. I think we should celebrate! You go home for Christmas in a few days, why don't we have a few prosecco's in here and then head to Cargo?"

"Cargo? What's that?" Cargo sounds like what we'd get in Glasgow for a weekends worth of alcohol? What the hell is she on about?

"Well babe, Cargo is a place where we single ladies like to go and drink to meet fancy real estate guys?"

"Real estate guys? No thank you hun, I do not want to meet a soul."

"Ok well we don't need to talk to them, but we do need a night out and it is ladies' night, so it's free drinks. You either drink free wine and talk to me, or drink free wine and talk to a tall dark and handsome stranger? What you say?"

"Ok then." I couldn't help but smirk. Even if I didn't want to I have to at least socialize. I don't know anyone here except Lottie and Billie, and Billie is travelling all the time so I need to do something about it.

Pouring two glasses of prosecco Lottie jumped onto the couch beside me. "let's play a game?"

"A game?"

"yes, we need to say every single thing our perfect guy would be?"

"Do we have enough time for that, ha ha?"

"well, probably not for yours. So, I'll go first. . .. I totally love a geek?"

a geek? What is she on about? "really?" god we were different, thankfully, at least she won't Tilly me then. Best not say that though.

"he has to be a bit awkward and need styled. Those types are my favorite then I can make him better and he'll be like this woman is a savior, look what she's done to me, I am a better man. And automatically the mother then likes you because she sees her son styled up smart and no longer the scruffy mess in a worn-out band t shirt."

"babe, I genuinely can't think of anything worse. Why would you ever want to put yourself through that. If a man can't look after himself, how is he ever going to look after you?"

"I like someone that needs me to take care of them, if he needs you there he'll always want you there. It's simple. I do have a confession though, I did once date a man that wore a Casio watch." She chuckled hiding her face and chugging her wine.

"A what?"

"A Casio watch? You know those calculator style watches?"

"I could honestly not think of anything worse! Oh my god Lottie, that is the biggest turn off ever! Another drink?" I poured two more drinks. "Where do I start. I need tall, above six feet tall, blue eyes, tanned or can tan well. I need tanned kids of course. Smart, funny, motivated, sorry not just motivated more motivated than me. So, my crazy ambitions don't sound so ridiculous. . ... What else, regular size feet, nothing too big and nothing too small. Someone that makes more money than me, not so I can have their money, more like so they can't have mine. Someone that gives me pet names and to an extend baby's me. But not in a creepy way. More of a cute caring way. Damian always called me gorgeous or monkey. One extreme to the other I know but it was our thing. . . "

I almost forgot where I was, Damian was four thousand miles away from me right now, with another "Gabriella" in his bed, in our home. Wow it was actually a lot to take in, everything I listed was him, he was my prince charming, the love of my life. He had the right sized feet and could make me laugh at the drop of a hat. I had never met anyone that took me the way he did, when I thought about it things had been tough since New York, something had changed and I never ever saw it. Was I so self-absorbed I let my own prince charming fall right through my hands?

"Gabby! Hello! Did you just describe Christian Bale in batman? Ha ha sharp suit, clean shave, fancy suit. Definitely not a Casio watch. Trust me, we are going to find these guys, maybe not tonight and maybe not next week. But we are on this journey together and like Ed Sheeran said Everything will be okay in the end, and if it's not okay it's not the end." For a moment, we sat in silence.

"Cheers! To us! Right let's get ready, which dress are you wearing?"

we both headed into our rooms to change for the night ahead. Lottie was a breath of fresh air, literally. I might not have been married but we both felt the same heartache and wanted to move forward no matter how hard it is to let go of the past and look forward, wherever forward was going to take us. And in our case looking forward was taking us to Cargo tonight.

I threw on my black and nude striped bandage dress and Jimmy Choo sling backs, I had less than fifty pounds in my purse but I certainly had to live up to the Dubai style even if it was only looks. Thank god, the drinks are free tonight. Dubai had certainly got one thing right with how to treat the ladies.

We got out of the taxi beside Dubai Marina, the yachts sprinkled the scenery each one bigger than the next. Cargo was restaurant/bar in a building called Pier 7. There was a restaurant/bar on each level and on a Tuesday night ladies could get three free drinks on every floor. How can girls even stand after that? There's no way we can actually handle that many drinks. The crowd was young professionals, some still in their suits from their day at the office and others flashing their Rolex watches and designer handbags looking like they are ready for a night on the town. The bar was loud and the music was bouncing. I had no idea people did stuff like this on a Tuesday night. If we were in Glasgow we would be watching coronation street with a cup of tea and a biscuit. Lottie ordered us our first drinks as I stood back to watch the people around me. This is a completely new world to me, I had to refrain from standing with my mouth open like a goldfish. Could I ever fit in here?

"Babe, here's your Cosmo, you can thank Cargo for that one! What is it we should cheers to? A new chapter?"

"To a new chapter!"

We had the perfect night out to finish the first leg of my new chapter. I was excited but couldn't wait to get back to my mum and Sophia in Glasgow, I needed a hug before I could do this.

Chapter 37

It wasn't too long before I was back in Glasgow, Bothwell was cold and crisp and the cold air hit my face as I walked Penny down the street for what was potentially one of the last times for the foreseeable future. The streets were coated with a thin white dewey topping and the place looked like a Christmas card. Christmas lights sparkled through the streets and everyone was busying around before the year was due to end.

I'd miss these streets, the small-town people with the big town attitude. The flash Harry's and the wannabes. The try hards and the everyday people that would wave to you in the street. I always thought I was a home bird, that I my kids would go to Bothwell primary like me and Sophia. That I could walk down the street with Lauren and our kids in their prams. I was giving up a lifetime of dreams for another dream that I lost when I met Damian.

I was the go getter, I was the overly ambitious know it all. The one who when she was told no worked ten times harder to make sure that she did it to prove everyone wrong. Even with Damian I was still very independent, just in a needy way. I didn't want to support myself, I wanted to do it as a team, I wanted to contribute to a better house, work harder for better cars and better holidays. Part of me was sad he wouldn't get it share this new chapter with me or be able to see what I'm really capable of. The funny thing is I still don't know who I'm trying to prove, my grandad always said if you can better yourself then do it.

I need to figure out the type of person that I am. Am I the hard-working housewife that juggles a fifty-hour working week and three kids? Or am I the cool auntie that lives abroad and brings home good presents? Did I want to live in a small cottage in Bothwell and do all those family orientated things? Or did I want to live in an apartment on the Palm? Did I want to dress in river island and top shop or did I want to have a wardrobe full of designer shoes? Ok I'll admit I always wanted the wardrobe full of shoes part. I wasn't committing to a lifetime in Dubai, I just need time to breath and decide which type of person I am and which type of life I should have. Raymond was amazing, he said if I wanted to go back to my old job I've to call him. I had to see myself as lucky, and luckily I didn't marry a lying cheating bastard, luckily I had an amazing family and friends to support me through such a massive decision, and lucky that I had security in my career if it doesn't go to plan in Dubai.

Christmas in our house is normally busy and full of chaos with the boys staying. Mum's Christmas eve party this year was more low-key and almost solemn. We glammed up and popped a bottle of prosecco before walking round to Da Luciano's with my auntie, my mum, David, and Sophia. Every step of the way I couldn't help but take in my surroundings, the shape of the concrete on the pavement, the trees that lined the streets connecting us to the main street in the town that was home. The church we sang in when we were at school and the paper shop I walked to with my dad on a Sunday when I was little. All the memories flooded my brain as we carried on walking with our jackets and scarfs wrapped around us tightly. The cold feeling, I wouldn't get living in the Arabian desert strangely comforted me. I remembered driving the SLK down the street with the top down in the summer with my uncle, and the shop we bought lunch in for my gran and grandad.

As we entered the bar the same faces we have known over the years greeted us. Soon I wouldn't know anyone.

"Heeeeeyyyyyy sisssssttaaaaaaaaaa! What ya thinking about?" David said putting his arm around me.

"Nothing much! Just gonna miss you all."

"We'll at least when we go partying it'll be in Dubai!!! Yeeeeeeeee boy!!!!!"

"I know it'll be fun." I downed my prosecco and held out for another glass.

"Gabby! Behave yourself! I'm not having you hungover in your bed all day tomorrow. We've got Christmas dinner tomorrow!" Mum said pouring my next glass.

"ok mum, love you!"

"love you too, I'm so proud of you. Just make the best of this opportunity."

As she finished speaking my gran entered the bar. I was lucky to have a family of good looking women that aged well. My gran was so glamourous, she was one of the closest people to me in my life. I was dying to squeeze her.

"Hello my girls!" she said grabbing us. "You both look gorgeous, shall we take one of those pictures? A selfie? Is that what you call it?"

She was one of these wonderful people that could be in anyone company. She was most happy when she was around us. Just like grandad said they never had four kids, they had six, me and Sophia too.

"Now I have more reason to come to Dubai all the time honey! Now go there and don't look back."

'Home will always be home gran."

"You're right, it always will be. But you're going to go so far you're not going to want to come back."

I loved her confidence, just like my mum they gave me strength. We drank and danced, and greeted the locals we've known all of our lives. Watching my mum and gran beam while telling people what I was about to do filled me with pride. I couldn't mess this up, not that there was much left to go wrong. But they had my back 100%. If I couldn't do this for me, I surely had to do it for them.

We stumbled back home a little after 1am and I slipped into my single bed with Penny lying on my back as usual, it's safe to say single beds suck. I can't wait to star fish in my new bed. I have a place to live in Dubai, did I just say that? I couldn't wait to get there.

In our usual routine Sophia and I burst out of bed early ready to unwrap presents and see the look on each other's faces with the thoughtfulness/craziness of what we'd bought each other. Mum put the music channels on in the background and made a full Scottish breakfast, we were like kids again. There was wrapping paper everywhere and presents covering each sofa. Even at the age of twenty-five I was still treated like a kid that believed in Santa. As I unwrapped my presents, I looked over at

Sophia and David. They were so in love and so good for each other. They were so good to me. They held me together, through the drunken nights out and the heartbreak of the century. I needed a moment alone. Damian loved this, he loved the effort at Christmas and loved sitting with us munching toast and having a beer with David in the morning. My heart sank as I realized he was doing this with her, and her family. Overwhelmed I headed for the bathroom. He's gone and this isn't a dream, Gabriella Johnson, you're moving to Dubai and you're going to forget all this ever happened. It was real, he left me in Vegas for her and he never contacted me again. What was I meant to do, call him and say Merry Christmas, please be sorry for what you did to me? That's not my way, and even if it was I could never embarrass myself to actually do it.

Five months of backwards and forwards. Laughter and tears, embarrassing moments and memories with people I will never forget. The end of Damian and Gabriella had brought me experiences and friendships I never thought I would've had, should he still have been in my life.

"G!!!!!! What are you doing in there!!' Sophia banged on the door. "I knew you'd be emotional today, we've cried for months about it, so why not today eh?"

She leaned on the other side of the door and began singing. "Turn around, every now and then I get a little bit lonely and you're never coming round. . .''

"Soph! Shut up I'm coming out!" She'd sung that song our whole lives, and by god was singing not her forte. "Can we just go eat dinner and get drunk?"

"Ok G, we'll do it, but don't ask me to hold you later!! HA!" only Sophia could make me laugh at probably what was the most humiliating thing after being dumped in Vegas. If you don't laugh you'll cry.

"Soph? can you hold me before we go face mum and David?"

"HA! Course ya sausage!" Sophia buried my head into her neck and gave me a tight squeeze. "I love you G, no matter what's happened or what is going to happen next. Just always be strong. If you can stand there and take that. You can handle anything. I love you k?"

"I love you too sis." I sobbed into her neck hoping no one would come through the door and see us. I wish she could come with me and protect me from whatever was going to be next. I wish she could live these new moments and experiences. I wish we were close friends like this before the exit of Damian. My sister became the most solid part of my world, nothing broke her down and nothing made her cry even though I could feel her anger towards the situation she stood with poise and presence. She handled everything like she was picking up milk at the shops and that nothing was difficult. She was the Beyonce in my world, she taught me how to be strong, and taught me to try again.

With a spinning head and heart full of laughs we walked back to mums. I Don't think I'll ever miss the cold weather? Or the rain? Would I?

"Did you have fun girls?" Mum said hugging us both into her.

"Yup!" I hiccupped.

"Last night in mum's house for a while?" Mum said while she poured a cup of tea and Sophia took a bottle of prosecco out of the fridge. "Now, on a serious note. I know your reasons and I understand it all. But if you want to come home at any point. Just come home. Everything will be ok. . ."

"I know, I just want to breathe that's all."

"I know darling, but if you don't want to come home. Just make sure you smash it! If anyone can do it its one hundred per cent you babes."

"I know it won't be easy, but like Sophia said, I've said my whole life I'm this independent person, and I need to show that now."

Half tipsy and gulping more prosecco in my house almost made reality shock me more. This time tomorrow I'll be in an apartment/hotel in Dubai, on my own.

"I think I need to get to bed mum. Long day tomorrow." As I kicked the remaining prosecco in the glass Sophia gave me a kiss.

"Sleep well G! and don't take any of my stuff to Dubai please."

I was surely going to miss them both, and David, and my gran and my whole family and my whole life actually. Thank god, I'd drank at least a bottle of prosecco. As soon as my head touches the pillow I'm going to fall asleep and forget about the butterflies in my stomach.

"Morning babes." Mum said passing me a cup of tea. "Are you ready for this?"

I nodded and took the tea from her hands. Penny snuggled against my back like she knew I was going.

"Sorry I can't take you to the airport, we have a really big meeting at work and I couldn't change it. Anyway, I don't want to make this an overly emotional good bye. So, I'll see you soon, okay babes?"

"See you soon mum. Love you."

"Always."

And that was it simple and without any drama, I'm moving to Dubai today and my mum will see me soon. Holy shit! I lay down for ten minutes and thought of everything I hadn't managed to fit in my case, my black over the knee boots – do I even need them anyways? My Mac? Probably not? I have bikinis, some day clothes, some night clothes and work clothes. Surely that will be enough. I didn't have time to mess around I showered, changed and put on a face of makeup. My head was in overdrive with the pros and cons of doing this. Wasting my opportunity at Porsche Glasgow, leaving my friends and family, Penny. Giving up on myself? Sitting in the taxi made everything so much more real. I needed a Sophia pep talk.

It was safe to say Damian leaving nearly killed me. I have to make this change and move forward. What else is there to lose?

The love of my life – check

My home – check

My sanity – check

My job – check

All of "our" friends – check

My ability to walk down the street – check

The ability to make it through a day without crying – check

I may not have a lot left but I can do this. I need to get out of here and start again. The life I always dreamed about had to be around the corner, it just had to be. As I walked into the Airport I contained my shaking by dragging my suitcase towards the Emirates check in area, this was it. With one thirty kilogram suitcase I checked into Glasgow airport with my one way ticket. Trembling I put my bag onto the check in desk.

A pretty red headed lady smiled at me. "Welcome to emirates, can you give me your passport? Which destination are you going to?"

"Dubai" I said nervously.

"Brilliant! Are you going on holiday?" she beamed.

"No, I'm moving." Forcing a smile, I held back the tears. I am moving to Dubai, given the circumstances this wasn't as tough as I expected, I have always wanted to do this. And in this circumstance, it's not like I have a choice, I need out of here. A new beginning was around the corner and this was the final step I had to make in Glasgow before this new journey started.

"Ok sweets, here is your passport and boarding pass, if you head to the right and go upstairs to the departure lounge. Good Luck!" as she smiled I took a deep breath and headed upstairs.

It's funny how life changes, with 2014 coming to an end. I was very single, very fragile but very determined. If she wanted what I had then can you imagine what she will want when she sees what I'll have there. We'll just need to wait and see I suppose.

Printed in Great Britain
by Amazon